A.H. Barford, Henry A. Tilley

English Spelling

SALZWASSER
VERLAG

A.H. Barford, Henry A. Tilley

English Spelling

1st Edition | ISBN: 978-3-75251-650-0

Place of Publication: Frankfurt am Main, Germany

Year of Publication: 2020

Salzwasser Verlag GmbH, Germany.

Reprint of the original, first published in 1868.

DICTATION LESSONS.

ENGLISH SPELLING

A SERIES OF

DICTATION LESSONS

For the use of Schools and Private Students

ARRANGED BY

A. H. BARFORD, B.A., F.L.S.

HEAD MASTER OF THE ST. MARYLEBONE AND ALL SOULS GRAMMAR SCHOOL

AND

HENRY A. TILLEY

VICE-PRINCIPAL OF HANWELL COLLEGE, MIDDLESEX

LONDON

LONGMANS, GREEN, READER, AND DYER

1868

PREFACE.

————◆◇◆————

THE PRESENT LITTLE WORK is intended by the Compilers
to be a handbook, by the use of which teachers may
put their pupils through a complete course of English
Spelling, according to the most approved mode of
teaching that art, viz. by Dictation. The words
given for practice are those which experience in the
correction of papers of candidates for public appoint-
ment, has shown to be the most liable to mis-spelling.
The sentences have been framed in a manner that
will best show the common meaning of the words to
be dictated, and, at the same time, either to convey
some useful truth or moral, or to cause the pupil to
think and distinguish.

In the spelling of inflected words, no particular
dictionary has been followed. It is assumed, that in
teaching 'English Spelling, as it is,' no better guide
could possibly be found than that afforded by the
leading articles of the 'Times,' and of other first-
rate journals, which represent the Intellect of the
day. With all words of disputed spelling, though

only one form is given, care has been taken that the one selected is that which is most in accordance with common usage, whenever that usage is not opposed to the derivation of the word, and the analogies of the language.

The system of giving false, although. phonetic, spelling to School-boys for correction is pernicious, and does away with all that assistance which the eye affords when any perplexity in the spelling of a word arises. The Compilers are of opinion, however, that the plan they have adopted at the end of the book, of giving selections from old authors for re-writing with modern spelling, will not have that objection : on the contrary, it is hoped that, the School-boy being now sufficiently sure of his spelling, such exercises will prove beneficial, by directing his attention to the various inflexional and orthographical changes which have really taken place in the English language.

CONTENTS.

———◦◇◦———

APPENDIX.

DICTATION LESSONS.

----◆----

INTRODUCTION.

A VIBRATION of the air coming in contact with objects produces various sounds.

A vocal sound is that vibration which is caused by the human organs of speech. Air is propelled from the lungs, and the sound so produced is modulated by the glottis, the roof of the mouth, the tongue, the teeth, the lips, and the nose.

Language is a combination of vocal sounds forming words, by means of which men communicate their thoughts to each other.

Orthoëpy is the harmonious utterance of such language, and is acquired by the ear.

Orthography is the art of writing correctly (that is, in accordance with the accepted manner of the day,) such language, and can only be acquired by constant practice and a knowledge of the etymology of a language. In phonetic languages the orthography ought to represent as nearly as possible the orthoëpy. The human voice has, however, so many modulations that written symbols often fail to represent them exactly. This is especially found to be the case when transferring words from one language to another.

There are few languages in which the orthography differs so much from the orthoëpy as in the English language. The reason of this is that the English language is made up of words derived from various other languages, ancient and modern.

The basis of the English language, like the source of the English people, is Anglo-Saxon. The Keltic, Scandinavian, Norman-French, Greek and Latin languages are only contributors, in a greater or less degree, to its vocabulary. Of these, the Norman-French alone has influenced its grammatical forms. The others have simply supplied it with words.

This varied constitution of the English language accounts for the imperfection of its alphabet, and the irregularities in its spelling.

1.—In the English language twelve distinct sounds are represented by five symbols called vowels, or by combinations of them, thus :—

á (Italian), in *ah! father.*
ā　　　　　in *fate, bait, great.*
ă　　　　　in *fat, matter.*
ä = *or*　　in *fall, haul.*
ē　　　　　in *be, feed, lead.* *
ĕ　　　　　in *bed, instead, leisure.*
ĭ　　　　　in *pin, pity, civility.*
ō　　　　　in *note, moat, smoke.*
ŏ　　　　　in *not, cotton.*
o = ü　　　in *prove.*
ŭ　　　　　in *but.*
ū = *oo*　　in *pull, bullock, woolly.*

2.—Four sounds are diphthong, expressed by the letter ī (y), and combinations of the above vowel letters, viz. :—

ī (y) in *wine, mind, fly, buy.*†

* Another sound of *e* might be added—that of the final *e* in such words as *glebe, recede.* In the Russian language this sound has a separate letter.

† In the Russian language our sound ī is written as a diphthong, *aú,* as pronounced.

eu (*ew*) in *feud, muse, suit, due.*

oi (*oy*) in *oil, voice, boy.*

ou (*ow*) in *house, fowl.*

3.—*Y* and *W* are either vowels or semi-vowels.

As vowels, $y = \bar{i}$ or $\breve{e}$; $w = u$.

As semi-vowels (or more properly as aspirated vowels), $w = oo$, as *will* (*oo-il*), French *oui* = *we.*

$y = \bar{e}$, as *yet* (*ee-et*), French *y* = *e.*

4.—Sixteen sounds (consonants) are called mutes, which may be arranged in pairs, according to their sharp or flat utterance. Thus :—

Sharp.	Flat.
p pat.	*b* bat.
f fat.	*v* vat.
t tin.	*d* din.
th thin (Saxon).	*dh* that (Saxon).
k kin (*kh*) khan.	*g* gin (*gh*) ghost.
s seal (*ts*) tsar.	*z* zeal (*dz*).
sh sure, shore.	*zh* azure.
tsh (*ch*) chest.	*dzh* (*j*) jest.

5.—Four sounds are called liquids, from their propensity of doubling themselves or combining with other consonants. These are, *m, n, l, r.*

6.—One sound is nasal, as *ng* in *King.*

7.—One sound is aspirated, as *h* in *hot, which.*

8.—One sound is trilled, as *r*, especially after *w*, as in *wreck.*

9.—These 41 sounds of the English language can be represented in writing by 23 out of the 26 letters of the alphabet. The other three signs, c, q, x, are therefore superfluous or redundant, and only necessary in the language to show the derivation of the word of which they form part. Thus :—

c = *s* before *e, i, y*, as *cell, city, mercy.*

c = *k* before *a, o, u*, or a consonant, as *cat, cot, cut, clot.*

c with *h* = *sh*, *tsh*, or *k*, as *Charlotte, church, cha-racter.*

q (always followed by *u*) = *kw*, as *queen* (*kween*).

x = *cs, ks, cks*, as *lax, lacs, lacks.*

10.—The following should be observed.

That *g* is always hard before *a, o, u*, and conso-nants, as *gat, got, gut, glad.* That *g* is generally soft, or pronounced like *j*, before *e, i, y*, as *gem* (ex. *get*) *gill*, a measure (ex. *gill*, of a fish). Compare *auger, anger, germ, gypsy, gyp* (a college servant.)

That when two consonants come together in the same sound or syllable—a flat mute *in sound* succeeds a flat mute or a liquid, and a sharp mute succeeds a sharp mute.   When, *in writing*, a sharp mute follows a flat mute or a liquid, or a flat mute follows a sharp mute, either the sound of the second is changed to harmonise with that of the former, or a vowel must be inserted between them, when the word acquires another sound or syllable.   Compare *stacks* and *stags*. In *stacks*—*k*, a sharp mute, is fol-lowed by another sharp mute *s*, and the two letters harmonise. In *stags*, *g* is a flat—but as *s* is a sharp, the *s* must either be pronounced as the corresponding flat *z*, or the vowel *e* must be inserted when the word becomes one of two sounds as *stag-es.*

The same process is seen in the formation of the past tense and past participle of verbs, *passed*= *past, stepped* = *stept, looked* = *lookt, worshipped* = *worshipt.*

Attention to these remarks will account for the many anomalies in English spelling, as well as the great number of homonyms in the language, and convince the student that it is only by constant practice in writing, and observation in reading, he can ever attain to correct spelling.

SECTION I.

SINGLE WRITTEN VOWELS AND THEIR VARIOUS SOUNDS.

Exercise 1.

The letter *a* has five sounds :—

á (Italian), as *father;* and in all foreign words, as *bravo, banana.*

ā (English), as *fate.*

ă (short), as *fat.*

ä = *or*, as *fall, swarm.*

à = *ĕ*, as *many, Thames.*

EXAMPLES.

He made the bad boy bare his arms. The waters abated, and the dove came not back to the ark. That tall man was in a great rage at his fall from the car. Bar the back gate. Halve the walnuts and almonds. Take care of that swarm of ants. Bravo! you shall all have your reward. A basket of bananas. That is rather a rare idea.

bard, pall, raft, salve, waver, many, mallet, marvel, after, affect, palace, paltry, aware, cigar, manna, allow, appal, pacha, regatta, Thames, ancient.

Exercise 2.

The letter *e* has two sounds :—

ē in *be, recede;* *ĕ* in *bed, redden.*

N.B.—The final semi-vowel *e* following a consonant lengthens the sound of that consonant as well as of the vowel preceding it.

EXAMPLES.

Be merry and **wise.** The **sere** and **yellow** leaf.
Will you **ever accede** to my **request?** His **style** was
replete with **elegance. Ever comely, ever blithe.**
You **impede** my **movements.** The **Belle** of the **village.**
Mere talk. **Fruitful glebe.** The **heretic adhered**
to his **heresy. Revere** your **parents.** A **clergyman** is
called a **clerk.**

recede, secede, effete, complete, austere, adhere,
obscene, gangrene, Nicene, obsolete, reverence, tene-
ments, simile, epitome, hereditaments.

Exercise 3.

The letter *i* has four sounds :—
ī a spoken diphthong, as *site, wine.*
ĭ as *sit, civil, iniquity.*
i = ē in foreign words, as *intrigue, police.*
i = *u* or *e* before *r*, in *fir, birch.*

EXAMPLES.

Sit still while I write a line to invite him to **dinner.**
Fir wood **easily ignites. Ships' rigging is** now made
of **iron wire.** He had **thirty** yards of **thin twine** to
his **kite.** The **invalid** was **fatigued** by **his** walk **in**
the **ravine. Engines** and other **machines. Granite**
is a hard rock. An **infinity** of **caprices.** An **intri-
guing mandarin.**

hit, rite, basin, valid, respite, ivy, icy, police,
grimaces, profile, cavil, miry, wiry, idyls, sinner,
sinecure, oblique, oblige, chemise, prestige, initials,
inability, imbecile, routine, magazine.

Exercise 4.

The letter *o* has four sounds :—
ō in *go, promote.*
ŏ in *got.*
ö = ü = oo in *move, prove.*
o = ŭ in *tongue, sponge, stomach.*

EXAMPLES.

Do not move from your abode. The wolves worried the donkey. I wonder who is wandering there. The monkeys were very docile. The foe was worsted more than once. Worsted stockings. The soldier was killed at his post by the frost. A foul tongue is the sign of a disordered stomach. The pommel of a saddle. Put the shovel in yonder hovel.

host, worse, cord, glove, bowl, moth, tomb, womb, dove-cot, sloven, cover, spongy, bosom, tolled, extolled, reprove, cozen, onion, sonorous, worship, colonel, attorney, sacerdotal.

Exercise 5.

The letter *u* has four sounds:—

ŭ as *butter*.

ü = *oo*, as *bullock*.

ū = *eu* diphthong, as *muse*, *acute*.

u = *i* or *e* in *busy* and before *r*, as *bury*, *surge*, *purloin*.

EXAMPLES.

Put more sugar in the pudding. A tuneful lute. He pushed him into a puddle. The island of Bute. Soft music. A dutiful son. A wasp stung the butcher. A puling infant. That stupid busy body intruded everywhere. Refulgent moon. Cool as a cucumber. The surge of the ocean.

gull, pull, delude, purge, puny, useful, surly, surely, gusty, annul, utter, ruby, ruin, purport, usurp, purloin, future, prudence, usury, unicorn, cuckoo, business.

Exercise 6.

W as a vowel is always joined to another vowel, as part of a written diphthong, as *bow*, *skewer*.

W as a semi-vowel is always at the beginning of
a syllable = *ū* = *oo*, as *weed* = *oo-eed*,
          sword = *s-oo-ord*.

The letter *y* has two sounds :—

y final = *ī* diphthong in monosyllables and accented syllables, as *try, defy.*

y = *ĭ ŏ* in unaccented final syllables, as *duty.*

y in the middle of words shows generally their
derivation from the Greek ; *y* = upsilon, and
is nearly always short.

EXAMPLES.

By and by I will **try** it. Let **duty** come before
everything. You may **rely** on my **complying** with
your wishes. **By the bye**, does he **dye** his whiskers ?
A **martyr** is one who suffers for his conscience' sake.
Satyrs and **sylphs** are read of in **myths.** Know ye
the land of the citron and **myrtle** ? The **gypsy**
showed **symptoms** of **hysterics.** The **sycamore** bent
over the **crystal** pool. An **abyss** of despair. The
Pyramids are in **Egypt. Porphyry** is found in the
Pyrenees. Lynch law.

stye, style, lyre, lynx, pyre, nymph, crypt, lymph,
hymn, hymen, hyssop, cymbal, gypsum, hyphen,
synod, dynasty, oxygen, hydrogen, labyrinth, hal-
cyon, presbyter, synonym, paralysis, gymnastics.

y as a semi-vowel always begins a word, as *yew* =
ee-ew.

See **you** the **yew** tree **yonder** ? In days of **yore.**
A stout **yeoman.** The **yule** log. Are **you** fond of
yachting ?

yoke, yearn, yawn, yeast, yawl.

SECTION II.

DOUBLE WRITTEN VOWELS IN THE SAME SYLLABLE, WITH THEIR SOUNDS.

Exercise 7.

aa = *á* Italian, in *Bazaar*.
aa = *ā* English, in *Aaron*.

EXAMPLES.

To **baa** like a sheep. **Balaam's ass.** The land of **Canaan. Bazaar** is the Persian for a market. **Baal** is the same as Bel or Belus, and means the sun. **Isaac,** the son of Abraham. A Hottentot's **Kraal**.

Exercise 8.

ae has properly two sounds,—as *Gaël*.
ae (the Greek *ai*), as *daemon, aesthetic*.
N.B. In these words the *ē* is generally substituted for *ae*, as *demon*.

EXAMPLES.

Michaelmas day. **Israel** is another name for Jacob. The Highlanders still speak **Gaelic. Aeronauts** are those who go up into the air in balloons. The **Maelstrom** is a dangerous whirlpool on the coast of Norway. **Aerolites** are meteors. An **Israelite** in whom was no guile. **Æsthetics** is the science which treats of the beautiful in nature. **Æschylus** was a Greek poet. The Roman **Cæsars. Mediæval. Athenæum.**

Exercise 9.

ai (**ay**) has three sounds :—
ai (**ay**) = *ā* (English) *day, maintain*.

$ai = á$ (Italian) *plaister*.
$ai = i$ diphthong, as *aisle*.

EXAMPLES.

What **ails** you? Throughout the long drawn **aisle**. An **airy** habitation. Green **baize** on the stairs. The **Corsair** is by Byron. **Arrayed** in white **raiment**. Wrap the **plaid** around you. The **villain** stole my **braided waistcoat**. **Maize** is Indian corn. The **prairie** was covered with **daisies**. Have you no **entrails?** The **bailiff** pulled down the **railings**. The statute of **Mortmain**. An act of **attainder**. The troops **maintained** their position, and finally **prevailed** over the enemy. The **laird** had two **bairns**.

lair, frail, gait, gaiety, straight, boatswain, wainscoat, waylay, caitiff, Britain, raisins.

Ao is found only in the word *gaol*, for *jail*, *gaoler*, &c. *Pharaoh* (Dean Alford), *Pharoah* ('The Times.')

Exercise 10.

au (aw) has four sounds :—
au, aw = $\ddot{a}$ = *or*, as *daub*, *hawk*.
au = $á$ Italian, as *draught*.
au = $\bar{a}$ English, as *gauge*.
au = $\breve{o}$ as *laudanum, cauliflower.*

EXAMPLES.

The **awl**, **saw**, and **auger** are carpenter's tools. Speak **audibly**. His **aunt** had **auburn** hair. A long **pause** ensued. **Awful slaughter**. A **haunch** of venison. He was **assaulted** during a **brawl**. **Laurel** leaves. The **Dauphin** began his life under favourable **auspices**. **Laudanum** is a tincture of opium. **Cauliflower** is a flowering cabbage. Broad and narrow **gauge** of railway.

laugh, daub, sauce, gaunt, sprawl, gauze, vault,

launch, staunch, laurel, haughty, avaunt, dawdle, austere, autumn, hawthorn, gaudy, nautilus, autograph, debauchery.

Exercise 11.

Ea has four sounds :—
ea = ē, as *each, beacon.*
ea = ĕ, as *bread, leather.*
ea = ā (English), as *pear, forbear.*
ea = á (Italian), as *heart.*

EXAMPLES.

The herd came lowing o'er the **lea.** Never **swear.** Throughout the length and **breadth** of the **realm,** a **dreadful dearth** carried **disease** and **death** to every **hearth.** There is no **real pleasure** in **vengeance.** The **sea** rolls in upon the **beach.** The **feast** of un**leavened bread.** That painter's **easel** was his only **treasure.** The **hearse** bore away the **deceased** from the **bereaved** parent's view. The **beadle** had the **measles.**

pea, eaves, sweat, shear, flea-bite, sheaves, yeast, weave, teaze, lease, heath, crease, wealthy, stealthy, zealous, beacon, pageant, leather, sergeant, earnest, weasel, jealousy, feasible, treacle, endeavour, treacherous.

Exercise 12.

Ee has two sounds :—
Ee = ē, as *eel, feed, guarantee.*
ee = ĕ, as *levee, committee.*

EXAMPLES.

An **eel-pie** house. The golden **fleece.** Pins and **needles.** The wind **veered** to the east. The girl **sneezed** three times. Tea and **coffee. Geese** swimming in a **creek.** The **leech** pulled up his **sleeves** and

proceeded to **bleed** the **peer**. They **careened** the vessel on the **lee** shore of the island. The **auctioneer leered** and **sneered** at the **seer**. No one was **freer** than he. The **queen's levee**.

soup-tureen, steel, spleen, lees, seethe, black beetle, succeed, rupee, marquee, agreeable, absentee, domineer, pioneer, redeemable, electioneering, gazetteer.

Exercise 13.

Ei has four sounds :—
Ei = *ē*, as *seize, either.*
Ei = *ā* (English), as *vein.*
Ei = *ī* (diphthong), as *height.*
Ei = *ĕ*, as *forfeit.*

EXAMPLES.

The horse **neighed** thrice. It was a **feint** to **deceive** his **neighbour**. He **seized** the **reins**. All **deceit** is **heinous**. Send me a **skein** of silk to mend my **veil**. **Deign** to hear us. A salmon **weir**. The **weird** sisters. The **heir received** his estates back from the **sovereign**. The **ceiling** fell down. I cannot **conceive** why you **inveigh** against **foreigners**. They were **inveigled** into the place. The Earl of **Leicester**. Island of **Madeira**.

sleigh, sleight-of-hand, leisure, freight, surfeit, heifer, reindeer, counterfeit, heigh-ho! Seine, Seidlitz, deceitful, surveillance, eider-down, kaleidoscope.

Example 14.

Eo has four sounds :— .
Eo = *ē*, as *people.*
Eo = *ĕ*, as *leopard.*
Eo = *ŏ*, as *gudgeon.*
Eo = *ō*, as *yeoman.*

EXAMPLES.

Pigeon pie. The **widgeon** is a wild fowl. The first **sturgeon** caught in the Thames is presented to the Queen. **George's** life is in **jeopardy**. A **puncheon** of rum. Dreary **dungeons**. The Spanish **galleons** were taken. A field marshal's **truncheon**. The **surgeon** received a blow with a **bludgeon**. His friends joined him at **luncheon**. A blotted **escutcheon**. The **yeomanry** of England.

Exercise 15.

Eu (Ew) has two sounds:—
Eu Ew—a proper diphthong, as *few, feudal.*
Ew = ō, as shew.

EXAMPLES.

Shew the lady into that **pew**. There are **few** **screw** steamers on the **Euxine** sea. Taming of the **shrew**. Oxen **chew** the cud. **Sew** that button on. The **newt** is a reptile. An iron **skewer**. Deadly **feuds**. The **sewers** of London. A **ewer** is a washing basin. He pronounced a **eulogy**. The **Eucharist**. An attack of **pleurisy**. From morn till **dewy** eve. **Neutral** ships.

Hew, lewd, shrewd, sewer, sewing, Shrewsbury.

Exercise 16.

Ey has four sounds :—
ey = ā in monosyllables and accented syllables, as *prey, convey, Eyre.*
ey = ĕ in syllables not accented, as *valley.*
ey = ē in a few words, as *key.*
ey = i diphthong at commencement of words, as *eye, eyot.*

EXAMPLES.

The **covey** of partridges became the **prey** of the hawk. The troops **obeyed** and fired three **volleys.** The **money** was **conveyed** across the **valley.** Justices in **Eyre.** The **chimneys** fell with a crash. **Eyry** means an eggery. The **Dey** of Algiers. **Ey** at the end of names of places means island, as **Alderney, Anglesey,** &c.

obey, storey, cockneys, parsley, attorneys, clayey, abeyance, abbey, honey.

Exercise 17.

Ia has two sounds, indistinctly merged into one, s *friar.*

N.B. To this class belong all words ending in *ial, ian, iant, iance.*

ia = *ă,* as *parliament.*

EXAMPLES.

A **phial** full of **Friar's** balsam. **Liars** are always shunned. A **fustian** coat. A **partial** eclipse of the moon. The **parliament** took the oath of **allegiance.** She was a **brilliant musician.** That **miniature** is an excellent likeness. **Briars** (briers) and brambles. **Martial** array.

cordial, ruffian, tactician, magician, financial, collegian.

Exercise 18.

Ie, ye = has three sounds :—

ie, ye = *i* diphthong, as *tie, dye, defies.*

ie, = *ē,* as *pier, cashier.*

ie, = *ĕ,* as *friend, families.*

To this class belong : 1st, plurals of nouns, the third person singular, present tense, and the past participles. of verbs ending in *y,* as *flies, pries, fried,* &c

2nd, participials ending in *ient*, as *sufficient*. 3rd, nouns ending in *ier*, as *hosier, cavalier*.

EXAMPLES.

He **grieves**, and finds no **relief** for his **grief**. A **sieve** of corn. That **ancient** castle stood a long **siege**. A **piercing** wind blew on the **pier**. Two **tierces** of wine. The **thief** was **reprieved**, I **believe**. A good **retriever**. The **soldier's niece shrieked**. A **mischievous** monkey. **Fiendish** laughter. The **liege** lord recovered the **fief**. **Transient** pleasures.

tier, bier, lief, shield, priest, wield, frontier, lien, mien, fiery, chieftain, osier, crosier, cashier, glazier, achieve, grievance, defies, deities, magpies, pannier, unwieldly, courtesies, proficient, capacities, magistracies, grenadier.

Exercise 19.

Io has two sounds, indistinctly merged into one.

To this class belong all words ending in *lion, nion, scion, sion, tion*.

ion = *yon*, or *shon*.

EXAMPLES.

Lambert Simnel was made a **scullion** in the king's kitchen. One **trillion**, two **billions**, three **millions**. He had a **bunion** on his toe. A sailor's **rations**. The king's **minions**. The **pinions** of a bird. An awful **collision**. The **trunnion** of a gun. **Onions** and leeks. A **coalition** was formed between the Whigs and Tories.

pension, contention, dissension, cushion, persuasion, aversion, dominion.

Exercise 20.

Oa has two sounds :—

oa = ō, as *oats*.

oa = ä = or, as *groat*.

The sturdy **oak.** A **loaf** of **coarse oaten** bread. The **boa** swallowed a **goat.** Eagles **soar.** A stupid **hoax. Hoarse croaking** of the frogs. I would not give a **groat** for it. Ships are calked with **oakum** and pitch. She had a **hoard** in the **cupboard.** The **foal** of an ass. The ancient Britons stained their bodies with **woad.** What an **uproar!** The **encroach-ments** of the enemy. **Noah's** ark.

boar, broad, coax, oath, roach, shoal, boatswain, bloaters, hoar-frost.

Exercise 21.

Oe has four sounds :—

oe = ō, as *foe.*

oe = oo, as *shoe.*

oe = ŭ, as *does.*

œ = ē (and written so), in some few words, as *phœnix, fœtid.*

To this class belong the plurals of substantives, and the third person singular, present tense, of verbs ending in *o,* as *cargoes, echoes.*

Hoe the ground around the **potatoes. Aloes** bloom but seldom. The **sloe** is a wild fruit. A **shoe-horn.** The death **throes** of the **roe** caused her a pang of **woe.** The cruisers seized several **cargoes** of **negroes.** The **heroes** of history. The **echoes** of the **grottos.** The price of **calicoes** is risen. A **fœtid** smell. The **phœnix** is a fabulous bird. His **manœuvres** were very clever.

toe, does (pl.), mangoes, chef d'œuvre, canoes, assafœtida, Phœbus, Phœnician.

Exercise 22.

Oi, oy, has a diphthong sound :—
Porpoise = porpus, as formerly spelt (Johnson).

EXAMPLES.

They divided the **spoils loyally.** He **purloined** a **sirloin** of beef. **Broiled oysters.** He was wounded in the **groin.** He **poised** the stick on his nose. **Porpoises** sport in **boisterous** weather. The **tortoise** was **poisoned. Anointed** with **oil** or **ointment.** Indian **soy.**

foil, moist, noise, joist, oily, jointure, allòy.

Exercise 23.

Oo has three sounds :—
oo = u in *cud,* as *blood.*
oo = u in *bull,* as *boot.*
oo = ō in *floor.*

EXAMPLES.

The **toothache.** Too much **soot** in the chimney. The **floor** was stained with **blood.** There are many **broods** of grouse on the **moors.** Othello the **Moor wooed** and won Desdemona. The **buffoon** acted in a **booth.** Have you been up in a **balloon? Loot** is **booty** taken in war. The **booby** is a stupid bird. The **baboon** and the **kangaroo** may be seen in the **Zoological** gardens. The **whooping** cough.

hoop, woolly, cooing, cuckoo, forsooth, sooty, oozing, rookery, gooseberry or gorseberry.

Exercise 24.

Ou (ow) has four sounds :—
Ou (ow) a diphthong *sound,* as *how, wound* (past t. of wind).

c

Ou (*ow*) = *ū* = *oo*, as *wound* (*subs.*) *bouquets.*
Ou (*ow*) = *ō*, as *soul, sowing.*
Ou (*ow*) = *ŭ*, as *rough, touch.*

N.B. To this class belong all words in *ous*, as *boisterous*, and most words from the Latin through the French in *our*, as *honour*, although the *u* is occasionally dropped in deference to the original deviation from the Latin.

EXAMPLES.

Now I **vow** I **know enough** of **you** to **vouch you would** not commit so **foul** a deed. Take the **dough** out of the kneading **trough**. They **followed** the **plough**, and **sowed** the seed in the **furrows**. A **soldier** on **furlough** was **carousing**. Sheep **browsing** on the **mountain's brow**. **Although** his **outside** was **rough** and **uncouth**, his **soul** was **thoroughly sound**. **Lough**, loch, or lake, means the same thing. The member for the **borough** rode in a **brougham**.

crow, crown, vouch, slough, drought, bough, lower, drowsy, doughty, poultice, sources, snowy, journeys, resource, rendezvous, vigour, honourable.

Exercise 25.

Ua has two sounds:—
Ua = *wa*, in *assuage, persuasion.*
Ua = *á* (Italian), as *guard*.   *Qu* = *kw*.

EXAMPLES.

Guarded language. Quails are birds. He **assuaged** the **qualms** of the **Quaker's** conscience. I was his **guarantee**. That **squall** did much injury to the **squadron**. He **squandered** his property in **squabbles**. The proceedings were **quashed**. They danced a **quadrille** in the **quadrangle**. **Guarantee.**

quart, quartz, quarto, quarry, dissuade, victuals.

Exercise 26.

Ue has two sounds :—
Ue = a diphthong sound, as *flue, revenue.*
Ue = *e,* as *guest, coquette.*
Ue final after *g* and *q* is silent, as *rogue, mosque.*
Qu = *k* or *kw.* *Gu* = *gw,* as *guelph.*

EXAMPLES.

His death was **due** to an **ague. Glue** is made from the sinews of animals. Can you **guess** how the **rogue** was **rescued?** He pronounced an **harangue** over the new **statue.** The **Huguenots** were French Protestants. His hands were **imbued** with blood. The parliament was **prorogued. Croquet** is much in **vogue.** The **mosque** is up the **avenue.** The **Basques** live in the Pyrenees. Queen Victoria is a **Guelph.**

sue, vague, argue, flue, plague, guest, lacquer, intrigue, oblique, antique, burlesque, etiquette. dialogue, retinue.

Exercise 27.

Ui (uy) has four sounds :—
Ui (uy) has two diphthong sounds in *suit, buy, guide.*
Ui (uy) = *ĭ,* as *guilt.*
Ui (uy) following *g* or *q* has a peculiar sound, as *quiver, anguish.* *Qu* = *kw, gu* = *gw.*

EXAMPLES.

The **guide** was **equipped** for the journey. A **quire** of paper. The **juice** of the **quince.** He is gone for a **cruise.** Judges on **circuit. Conduit** Street. What a **guy** he looks with that **guitar!** The Roman nose was **aquiline.** The perfume of the **jonquil** is **exquisite.** Did you ever ride in a **palanquin?** Don **Quixote** was written by Cervantes, a Spaniard.

Quizzed, disguise, guile, guinea, bruised, biscuit, sluice, nuisance, pursuit, recruit, quiver, roguish, juicy, squirrel, mosquito, perquisite, equilibrium.

Exercise 28.

Uo is found in a few words only, and is pronounced *ō* or *ŏ*, as, more *liquor, quoth* he. He *quotes* poetry. What is the *quotient* of that sum ?

Three vowels in the same syllable have usually a diphthong sound, as *view, buoy, eye.*

EXAMPLES.

A nearer **view** showed how the **eye** could be deceived. A game of **quoits.** A **ewe** lamb. A **buoy** marked the spot of the wreck. The **lieutenant** fell over a gun **quoin. Buoyant** substances. The **lacquey** walked on the **quay.** The **Saviour** of the world. Lord Byron's poem of the **Giaour** (Djoor). **Gracious behaviour. Nauseous** medicine. A **gorgeous** sunset.

liver, sewer, quaint, squaw, squeeze, squeak, skewer, luscious, squeamish, conscious, religious, facetious, conscientious, sacrilegious, &c.

Exercise 29.

Words arranged according to sound, for practice by dictation.

A in father.

half	psalm	martyr
chaff	heart	sarcasm
laugh	mart	cigar
raft	aunt	bazaar
quaff	guard	guitar
giraffe	scarred	catarrh
calm	almond	pacha
barm	rascal	barbarous
qualm	bravo	arsenic

A in *fāte, brain, membrane.*

air	feint	invade
dare	bays	inveighed
tear	raise	retrograde
sware	main	chilblain
paired	maize	heinous
scared	tame	neighbour
bared	chaise	raiment
stairs	weighs	sovereign
staring	despair	arrayed
bane	declare	counterpane
vein	erase	champagne
swain	crazy	campaign
neighs	upbraid	expatiate
brays	weighing	opaque
baize	inveigh	librarian
skein	corsair	arraigned
saint	unawares	bayonet

Exercise 30.

A in *fat.*

sad	traffic	knapsack
plaid	cabal	mattress
abbot	harangue	manage
adage	alcohol	parallel
balance	algebra	pharisee
cabin	calibre	valiant
damage	chalice	assassin
hatchet	gallery	battalion
waggon	salary	bachelor

A in *fall.*

tall	talk	gauze
crawl	salt	vault
squall	chalk	wharf
Saul	stork	floored

gored	froth	assault
poured	broth	exhaust
sword	hawser	marauder
reward	laundry	appalling
hoard	stalking	bedaubed
adored	uncorking	autograph
worn	tawdry	orthodox
warning	gaudy	ornament
saunter	gorgeous	audibly
off	awning	marauder
cough	naughty	nausea

Exercise 31.

E in *be.*

cheese	retrieve	besiege
fleas	bereave	piercing
freeze	relieve	beetle
lees	thieving	beadle
seize	impede	wheedle
brief	proceed	revere
heaves	secede	intrigue
grieves	succeed	arrears
weaves	intercede	austere
peach	recede	adhere
screech	supersede	besmear
niche	fœtid	cashier
leek	conceit	caprice
fiend	replete	hyena
pique	concrete	plebeian
niece	discreet	Chinese
wreak	secrete	Japanese
squeak	counterfeit	guarantee
wield	teasel	mandarin
weave	weasel	grenadier
believe	measles	assignee
deceive	weevils	secrecy

E in *met, heifer, meadow, steady.*

red	spend	eligible
said	sweat	jealousy
bread	wren	alleging
guest	leisure	coquette
blessed	measure	lieutenant
meant	weapon	leopard
wealth	benefice	jeopardy
wreck	element	precipice
friend	effigy	venomous

Exercise 32.

Sound of *e,* (*ea*), *i, o, u, y,* before the letter *r.*

earl	search	herding
girl	sperm	hurdle
furl	worm	burglar
pearl	firm	curly
urge	dirt	purloin
surge	wort	sirloin
dirge	spurt	circuit
merge	churn	surly
scourge	chirp	certain
her	earth	curtain
fir	worth	surface
myrrh	mirth	disturb
purr	urgent	turbid
learn	converse ·	murmur
spurn	coerce	emergent
yearn	disperse	mirth
tea-urn	re-imburse	mermaid
herb	early	purser
hearse	sturdy	mercer
worse	wordy	inert
purse	girdle	urchin
birch	curdle	earnest
lurch	circling	journey

sojourn .	hirsute	termagant
adjourn .	Hercules	extirpate
urgent	detergent	perquisite
irksome	turbulent	liturgy

Exercise 33.

I, diphthong, in *wine*.

eye	height	finite
sigh	might	tyrant
tie	sleight	island
buying	indict	cypress
vying	sprightly	irony
dyeing	contrite	viscount
sighing	blithely	asylum
thine	miry	beguile
sign	fiery	disguise
condign	wiry	horizon
repine	mity	hyacinth

O in *note*.

owe	coax	bloated
sew	cloaks	quoted
toe	smokes	lonely
flow	hoax	mouldy
beau	soul	yeoman
toad	toll	soldier
rode	foal	cocoa
lowed	bowl	oakum
hoed	mole	bureau
woad	shoal	brooches
ore	whole	cockroaches
swore	control	encroaching
door	moan	photograph
soaks	throne	onerous
pokes	grown	ominous

Exercise 34.

O in *ŏn, nŏt.*

dog	frolic	gudgeon
dot	solace	dungeon
knob	vomit	escutcheon
yacht	novice	luncheon
nock	ostrich	pinion
watch	lozenge	minion
notch	lottery	cushion
cottage	policy	fustian
college	pigeon	bunion
comet	widgeon	colonist
forest	surgeon	botany

O in *move.*

prove	soup	saloon
proof	shrewd	uncouth
broom	shoed	untruth
cool	truce	ruthless
crew	wound	booty
crude	swooned	whirlpool
rule	tomb	tattoo
rood	balloon	taboo
smooth	canoe	cooing

U in *pull.*

pulling	bullion	bouquet
bullock	cuckoo	truant
woolly	sugar	tourist
youthful	courier	ruinous
bulwark	rhubarb	

Exercise 35.

U in *tub.*

buzz	shunned	double
come	monk	bubble
dumb	drudge	sulphur
glove	tough	luggage
lungs	courage	dovecote
sponge	cupboard	monkey
wrung	couple	mongrel
young	cozen	luxury
tongue	stomach	attorney

Eu in *feud.*

use	refuse	neutral
hew	ensues	newspaper
you	peruse	nuisance
due	pursues	beauteous
ewe	diffuse	cucumber
sue	Jewish	glutinous
gnu	juicy	feudalism
lieu	gluey	revenue
feud	sinewy	suitable
lewd	pewter	putrefy
nude	puny	utensil
hewed	shrewd	usury
stewed	brewed	musical
viewed	elude	amusement
rued	sluice	municipal
news	obtuse	pneumatics
cruise	intrusive	circulate
brews	feudal	credulity

SECTION III.

HOMONYMS, OR WORDS PRONOUNCED EXACTLY ALIKE, BUT HAVING DIFFERENT MEANINGS.

THE great difference between the sound and the spelling of so many words in the English language may be thus explained:

1st. Because of the many combinations of vowel signs to which the same sound is given, as seen in the following words:— *corse, coarse, course; eve, leave, believe, perceive, retrieve, bereave,* &c. *See ex.* 1-28. The unison of sound of *e, i, o, u, y* before the letter *r,*—thus, in *her, fir, word, fur, myrrh,* in all which the vowel sound is the same. *See ex.* 32.

2nd. Because there are so many silent consonants, or consonants having similar sounds, as *site, cite, sight; lacks, lax, lacs; draft, draught; ascent, assent; nor, gnaw. See ex.* 83-89. The unison of sound of *le* with *al, el, ol, ul, yl. See ex.* 103-104.

3rd. Because (as has been explained in the Introduction) a sharp mute, in speaking, must be followed by a sharp mute, and a flat mute by a flat mute, whereas, in writing, a sharp often follows a flat, or *vice versâ,*—thus: *tracked, tract; tacked, tact; passed, past,* &c.

4th. Because the accent on a syllable doubles the sound of the final consonant, and carries it on to the succeeding syllable. This is especially seen to be the case with the liquids *m, n, l, r*—thus: *canon, cannon; palace, Pallas; panel, impannel; aloud, allowed,* &c. *See ex.* 79-82.

N.B. Numerous words usually classed as homonyms are in reality only such when pronounced by careless speakers. Exercises on these will be given in the section following.

Exercise 36.

He **adds all** together. A cooper's **adze** and a cobbler's **awl.** The **arc** of a circle. Noah's **ark.** It is not **allowed** to speak **aloud.** For **aught** I know you **ought** to do it. What **ails** you? The **ascent** is steep. Do you **assent** to it? Burton **ales.** A fine **air. Ayr** is a town in Scotland. Leeds is on the river **Aire. Ere** he went away. **Whene'er** I go. **Whate'er** I see. **Where'er** I roam. He was **heir** to that estate. Justices in **Eyre.**

Exercise 37.

Eight times 8. An **ait** or eyot is a river island. I'll take a walk up the **aisle** of the church. The **Isle** of Man. Cain and **Abel.** Are you **able** to do it? An **auger** is a tool. That **augurs** badly for the future. His **aunt** sat down on an **ant** hill. Are you going to alter the **altar?** An **annalist** composes annals. He was a celebrated **analyst.** Go into the **anteroom.** The **Anti-Christ.** An **antimacassar. Antediluvian.**

Exercise 38.

He could not **bear** to wear **threadbare** clothes. He **bares** his back, which **bears** signs of many stripes. Black **bears.** That **bald** man **bawled** out that he was **black-balled.** The wind **bows** down the **boughs** of the trees. A diamond **brooch. Broach** that cask. A wild **boar.** A **boa-constrictor.** What a **bore** he is! The rude Carinthian **boor.*** The carpenter **bored** a hole in the **board.** That lady has lost her **boa.**

---

* Or onward, where the rude Carinthian boor
Against the homeless stranger shuts the door.
GOLDSMITH.

Though the sky was **blue**, the wind **blew** strongly.
A **beech** tree stood near the **beach**.

Exercise 39.

By and by you must **buy** me some paper. **By the bye**, I have forgotten something. I'd **be** a busy **bee**. Have you **been** in the **bean** field? Don't **beat** me. **Beet-root. Beys** are Turkish officers. **Bay** trees. Green **baize**. Do not **bate** the price. Horses taken in to **bait**. A **bale** of goods. The prisoner was **bailed**. They **baled** the water out of the boat. The stag **breaks** through the **brake**. **Bread** and cheese. A **thorough-bred** horse. A **bass** voice. Such a **base** action. **Bows** and arrows. The **beaux** and **belles** of the village. Merrily the **bells** are ringing.

Exercise 40.

Strong **beer** brought him to his **bier**. A **birthday**. Have you taken your **berth** in the steamer? The **boy** clung to the **buoy** but all in vain. A **butt** of sherry. Rams **butt**. The **bite** of a mad dog. **Bight** or bay of Benin. The ass **brayed**. Maidens **braid** their hair. **Balmy** air. **Barm** is yeast. Oak **bark** is used for tanning. A **barque** of 300 tons. He **brews** every October. A **bruise** is a contusion. Let the dead **bury** their dead. The **berry** of the elder tree. A **breast** of veal. **Brest**, a seaport in France. The **Borough** of Marylebone. Rabbits **burrow** in the earth. A large **bridal** party. There is only a **bridle** path. A **Baillie** is a Scotch officer. The Old **Bailey**. John **Bunyan** is the author of the Pilgrim's Progress. He had a **bunion** on his toe.

Exercise 41.

Do you **call** that thing a **caul**? Always **check** your **cheques**. He sent the boy for ten **cents'** worth of **scent**. Do not throw the **sealing** wax at the **ceil-**

ing. **Coal** and iron are the sources of England's wealth. **Cole** means cabbage; whence **cauliflower** and **brocoli.** A goodly apple, rotten at the **core.** The Royal Marine **Corps. Corse** is another word for **Corpse.** Of **course** you can use **coarse** cloth. A splendid **courser.** This stuff is much **coarser** than that. The **colonel** cracked the nuts and ate the **kernels.**

Exercise 42.

The **cork** tree grows in Spain. They **calk** ships with pitch and oakum. A **cask** of Madeira. The horseguards wear **casques** or helmets. A hermit's **cell.** Do you **sell** celery? The cow **chews** the cud. **Choose** which you like. A hempen **cord.** The **chord** of the lyre. All the rooks **cawed. Cit** is an abbreviation for citizen. **Sit** down. A good building **site.** What a glorious **sight!** I shall **cite** you to appear. A **clause** in the will. The cat's **claws. Clime** of the unforgotten brave. **Climb** yonder pole. A **creek** is a small tidal river. Your boots **creak.** The rook **caws;** what can be the **cause?** A billiard **cue.** Give me the **cue** of your part. People once wore **queues** or pigtails. Mind your p's and **qu's. Kew** is famous for its botanical garden.

Exercise 43.

The **sere** and yellow leaf. A wise man was once called a **seer.** His face was **seared. Cerecloth.** Two bushels of **seed. Cede** it to him. **Clew** up the sails. They found the **clue** to that mystery. Idols **carved** in stone. The cow **calved** yesterday. Lord Warden of the **Cinque** ports had orders to **sink** the enemy's ships. The third **session** of Parliament. The **cession** of the Ionian Islands. My **candid** opinion. **Candied** lemon peel. **Cereals** are grain-bearing plants.

Serials are periodical literature. **Caudle** is a drink. A **caudal** appendage. The boats' **crews** went off for a **cruise**. The widow's **cruse** of oil. Sails are made of **canvas**. To **canvass** for votes. **Carcase** means a dead body, **carcass** the case of a rocket. The **cannon's** opening roar. **Canons** of the Church. Don't be **cast** down. He was a **half-caste**. **Coin** of the realm. A gun **quoin**.

Exercise 44.

The **Dey** of Algiers appeared every **day** at his divan. The **Dane disdained** the German's proposal. **Deign** to hear me, my Lord. **Dost** thou think he will lick the **dust** from thy feet? When is that bill **due**? The **dew** is on the grass. He quaffed the **draught**. His **draft** was dishonoured. That **doe** is of a **dun** colour. The **dough** is not **done** enough. The beavers **dammed** up the stream. **Damned** means cursed. Oh, **dear** me! The **deer** is **dying**. They are **dyeing** the cloth. He was a **dyer** by trade. A **dire** calamity. Three scruples make a **drachm**. He does not scruple to drink a **dram**. Two bucks and three **does**. Go and have a **doze**.

Exercise 45.

I cannot see anything in your **eye**. That man can **earn** eighteen pence a day. Can storied **urn** or animated bust? Bring up the **tea-urn**. When the **fourth** prisoner came **forth** he seemed to **faint**, but it was only a **feint**. I would **fain** do it, if I could. Never **feign** illness. Apollo's **fane**. What is the **fare** to Leipsig, for I am going to the **fair** which is held there. The bird **flew** into the **flue** of the chimney. Did you **find** it? He was **fined** £5. The **fore** mast of a ship. **Four** or five **fawns**. **Fauns** and satyrs. They **flee** away. Only a **flea-bite.** A **foul** deed. Domestic **fowls.** What a pretty **flower**! **Flour** is ground corn. A hard **fate.** At the last **fête** a man performed a remarkable **feat** with his **feet.** An **effete** population. Tilbury **Fort.** Sketching was his **forte.** A forest of **firs.** Animals with warm **furs.** The deer bounded through the **furze** bushes. Swiftly **flows** the river. **Floes** are masses of drift ice. Numerous **frays** took place among the clans. Repeat that **phrase.** He **frees** his country. Does it **freeze**? **Frieze** is a coarse kind of cloth. **Philip** gave him a **fillip** on the ear. I always **filter** the water. A **philtre** is a love charm.

Exercise 46.

Open the **gate.** What an awkward **gait**! He confessed his **guilt.** The watch was only **gilt.** My **guest guessed** the riddle directly. None **greater** than he. Give me the nutmeg **grater.** He threw down the gauntlet as a **gage. Greengages.** Broad and narrow **gauge** of railway. Bitter as **gall. Gaul** is the old name of France. To **gild** the ceiling. A **guild** is a company of merchants, whence **Guildhall.** Throw that **great** piece of dirt into the **grate.** He still **grieves** for his child. **Greaves** were armour for the legs. How he is **grown**! Pray don't **groan** in that manner. A **grocer** is one who sells things *en gros*, or wholesale. A **grosser** mistake I never heard of. Bears' **grease.** The isles of **Greece.** It cannot be disguised that those who go about with **Guys** on the 5th November are in **guise** greater **Guys** than the **Guys** they carry. Poor **Guy Faux**, or **Fawkes.**

Exercise 47.

The doctor says he'll **heal** my sore **heel** in a week. A **hale** old man. **Hail** stones. **Haling** men and

women. It is **hailing** hard. **Hail**, master! **Hail**
that **Hansom** cab. What a **handsome** man! Did ye
not **hear** it? **Here** I am. The Golden **Horde** of
Tartars had an immense **hoard** of corn. Is your
name **Hugh**? **Hew** it down, and cast it into the
fire. The **hues** of the rainbow. **Hie** thee away.
Although **high**, its **height** is not extraordinary.
Childe Harold, was he **hight**. What a noble **horse**!
The boatswain bawled till he was **hoarse** to **haul**
the cable through the **hawse** hole. A baronial **hall**.
My **heart** is in the Highlands. As pants the **hart**
for cooling streams. Ask **him** to sing that **hymn**.
He **hoes** the ground. Three pairs of cotton **hose**.
Plying for **hire**. **Higher** than the angels. Brush
your **hair**. **Hare** skins. That **harebrained** fellow
had a **hair-breadth** escape.

Exercise 48.

The **Inn** is in the High Street. The **Inns** of Court.
Innsbruck means bridge over the **Inn**. Raspberry
jam. Don't **jamb** your fingers. A **jury** of your
peers. **Jewry** means an assemblage of Jews. Old
Jewry is a street in London. **Jane** wore a dress
made of **jean**. Don't **incite** another to mischief. I
had an **insight** into his affairs. He **inveighed** against
every one who dared to **invade** his rights. **Idle** men
make pleasure their **idol**. The author who **indited**
that work was **indicted** for libel.

Exercise 49.

He **led** me to the **lead** mines, in which the **lodes**
of ore were very rich. The cows **lowed** whenever a
load of hay went by. A **lode-stone**. The **leek** is a
vegetable. That ship has sprung a **leak**. **Lear** is a
man's name; **Leah** a woman's. Don't **leer** in that
manner. The **links** of a chain. He had the eyes of

D

a **lynx.** A lion's **lair.** The **layer** of mortar was too thick. **Lo!** it is I. He was **laid low.** Don't **lade** the ship too deeply. The falling **leaf.** I'd as **lief** do it as not. **Lean** on me. He had a **lien** on the goods. **Lean** meat. Come o'er the **lea** with me. A **lee** shore. Shun a **liar.** With flying fingers touched the **lyre.** That man had **lain** a long while in the **lane.** A poor **lone** woman asked me for the **loan** of sixpence. You **laud** that **lord** more **loudly** than good sense **allows.** **Lie** still. **Lye** is the solution of an alkali. Sound in every **limb.** Painters **limn** their subjects. **Lax** in his principles, he **lacks** also perseverance. **Shell-lac** is a kind of gum. Ten **lacs** of rupees. A **levy** of troops. The Queen seldom had a **levée.**

Exercise 50.

The little **maid made** her **mantle,** and put it on the **mantel-piece,** when she was **dismayed** on seeing it take fire. The blood **mantles** to her cheek. The first-born **male** child was slain. A coat of **mail.** The **mail** train. **Mainsail.** That is the **main** point. Comb the horse's **mane.** The boundless **main.** The field **marshal** complimented the men on their **martial** appearance. The Lord of Hosts shall **marshal** us. **Mangel** is a root resembling beet. What is the price of that **mangle?** His body was horribly **mangled.** A flowery **mead.** Darius the **Mede.** Are you fond of **mead?** **Meed** is something merited. A **mean** action merits contempt. A steady **mien** and a calm **demeanour.**

Exercise 51.

A **moan** proceeded from the **new-mown** hay. Power and **might.** The poor widow's **mite.** **Mighty** actions. **Mity** cheese. A **maze** is a labyrinth. **Maize** is Indian corn. A **mote** in the eye. Surrounded by a **moat**. A stubborn **mule**. What animals **mewl**? We **missed** him in the thick **mist**. The **Lord Mayor** had the **night-mare**. What **metal** is that? His horse was full of **mettle**. Don't **meddle** with what does not concern you. He wore a Crimean **medal**. She is a great **meddler**. The **medlar** is a fruit. Raw **meat**. When shall we **meet** again? **Mete** out justice to all. A new **mode** of doing things. They soon **mowed** the grass. That is **mere** pretence. A **meer** is a small lake, sometimes spelt **mere**, as **Windermere**. **Mark** that man. A letter of **marque**. The tuneful **muse**. The cat **mews**. **Mews** are stables. Flesh and **muscle**. The **Mussulman** would not eat the **mussels**. A **missel** thrush. A **missal** is a Roman Catholic Prayer Book. Under the **mistletoe** bough. In what **metre** is that poem written? In the **gas-meter**. **Mucus** is a secretion of the **mucous** membrane.

Exercise 52.

No one can **know** what I suffered. Neither he **nor** I. Did the mouse **gnaw** the cheese? They are repairing the **nave** of the church. What a **knave**! Are you in **need**? **Knead** the dough well. The **knell** of parting day. **Nell** is a woman's name. **Naps** are short slumbers. He **knaps** the spear asunder. It was a **knotty** question whether or **not** to cut the Gordian **knot**. **None** of the **nun's** friends **knew** her in her **new** dress. The **gnu** is an animal. **Nay**! don't say so. Horses **neigh**. Marshal **Ney**. A long **nose**. Who **knows** it? **Ayes** and **noes**. That play is given **nightly**. A **knightly** manner. He set him at **nought**. What a **naughty** boy.

The great and little **Ouse** are English rivers. **Ooze** is soft mud. The splash of the **oar** resounded **o'er** the water. Rich copper **ore**. **Oh**! I forgot, I **owe** you a shilling. **One** or the other **won**. **Aught** means any-

·thing. You **ought** to have told me you **owed** the money. Collins' **Ode** to the Passions. Will you **pare** a **pear** for me ? I want a **pair** of trousers **repaired.** Let us **repair** thither. The birds were **pairing.** They were **paring** the fruit. **Peeling** potatoes. The bells were **pealing** merrily. It did not **appear** whether or not the **peer** was on the **pier.** A **pier**-glass.

Exercise 53.

Don't **pore** so long over that book. **Pour** out the Samian wine. **Porous** earthenware. The **pores** of the skin. **Praise** the Lord. The wolf **preys** on the flock. He **prays** fervently. Paul **pries** to know if Peter has gained the **prize.** The **pall** was put over the coffin. **Saltpetre** is nitre. A valuable **pearl** fishery. **Purl** is a drink. **Pause** before you reply. The bear has huge **paws.** He climbs the greasy **pole.** The **poll-tax.** A **pole-axe.** A barber's **pole.** Out of the **pale** of the church. A milk **pail.** He has a **pain** in the head. A **pane** of glass. **Peace** be with you. A **piece** of cloth. The **Peak** is in Derbyshire. She did it out of **pique.** Give **place** to better men. **Plaice** is a flat fish. Vast **plains.** A **plane** is a geometrical figure and also a carpenter's tool. Very **plain** features. **Please** don't do that. The court of Common **Pleas.** He **picks** the best men. **Picts** and Scots. As he lay that night on his **pallet** of straw. A painter's **palette.** Does that wine suit your **palate** ? **Plait** that straw. The **grass-plat** (plot). The **pleats** of a shirt. He **completes** his 20th year to-day. A **pannel** is a sort of rough saddle. The **panel** of a jury.

Exercise 54.

Four **quarts** make a gallon. Gold is found in **quartz.** A **quire** of paper. The **choir** consisted of 400 persons. I'll be **queen** of the May, mother.

Quean means a disreputable woman. The **rubric** is so called because printed in **red** letters. He **read** badly ; he can **read** better if he chooses. A broken **reed. Wrapped** up in paper. **Rapt** in astonishment. I **rapped** three times at the door. **Rye** bread. Don't make **wry** faces. A heavy shower of **rain.** The **reign** of Queen Anne. Keep a tight **rein** on that horse. How do you spell **ranedeer ?** * He was **arraigned** for high treason. **Raining** hard. The **reigning** monarch. He wants **reining** in a little. Gird my **reins,** Oh, Lord ! Before he **reached** the end of the voyage, the poor **wretch retched** violently.

Exercise 55.

Some of us **rode** along the **road,** the others **rowed** up the river. The white **rose** and the red. He **rows** well. The **roes** of fishes. The **rays** of the sun were so powerful that he could not **raise** his eyes. The Emperor ordered them to **raze** the city to the ground. Shall you **roam** this year as far as **Rome? Roan** colour. The river **Rhone.** You are **right.** The last funeral **rite.** The **shipwright** can **write** well. **Rites, wrights, writes. Ring** the bell. Don't **wring** your hands. **Rung, wrung.** What is that **root?** There are several **routes** to Paris. **Rough** weather. You have lost your **ruff.** The **rustle** of the leaves. Lord John **Russell.** To **wreak** vengeance on one's enemies. Did he not **reek** with blood and smoke? The **rack** has long been unlawful in England. **Wrack** and ruin.

Exercise 56.

For **sale,** a quantity of old **sail** cloth. The man was scarcely **sane** to throw himself into the **Seine.** Can you **skate ?** An abundance of **scate** in the mar-

* Not **reindeer, or raindeer.**

ket. It **seems** to me that the **seams** of your coat are undone. Hooper was burnt at the **stake**. A capital beef **steak**. I'll **stake** my word on it. He was **sore** afraid. The lark **soars** to heaven. That **sore** will not heal. Hark! how she **sighs**. What **size** are your gloves? **Size** is glue. A man's **skull**. To **scull** a boat. **Shear** your sheep, do not flay them. **Sheer** ignorance. The ship **sheers** off. A pair of **shears**. The rock-beaten **surf**. Emancipation of the **serfs**. A **slight** mistake. The wizard performed some **sleight-of-hand** tricks. Money is the **source** of much evil. Mint **sauce**. A dress of **serge**. The **surge** of the ocean. He was **seen** three times. What a glorious **scene**! A **seine** is a sort of fishing net.

Exercise 57.

He **sees** his error. Orders to **seize** all ships on the high **seas**. To **seise** and **disseise** are legal terms. Brevity is the **soul** of wit. His **sole** resource. The **sole** is a fish. How are they **sold**? My boots are newly **soled**. A good **sign**. A **sine** is a line in geometry. To **slay** with the sword. A **sleigh** is the same as a sledge. What a **slow** coach! The **sloe** is a wild fruit. A **sower** went forth to **sow**. To **sew** on a button. The seamstress **sewed** from morn till night. Mr. **So and So**. **So** you cannot do that **soon**. Some **steel** filings. Thou **shalt** not **steal**! Go up **stairs**. How she **stares** at you! What a sweet **style** of expression! I cannot get over the **stile**. He was an ardent **suer**. The **sewer** empties into the Thames. An only **son** of his mother. The earth moves around the **sun**. I **sought** long to find one of the right **sort**. She turned her head on one **side** and **sighed** deeply. What a **staid** person! She **stayed** two hours. **Subtler** than all the beasts of the field. He was a **suttler** about the camp. Don't take such long **steps.** The **steppes** of Russia. **Sprite,** a spirit, is sometimes spelt **spright.** **Storks** are common in Holland. The **stalks** of a plant. He **stalks** the deer. Can **storied** urn or animated bust, &c. Build me a **three-storeyed** house. It is a long **story.** He lives in the top **storey.** A pig-**sty.** How do you spell **sty, (stye)** in the eye? The proper manner, according to derivation, is **stigh.** A bundle of **sticks.** The river **Styx.**

Exercise 58.

A tropical forest **teems** with life. He drove **teams** of fine horses. Have you heard the **tale** of the fox who lost his **tail** in a trap? They **tied** the girl on the shore when the **tide** was coming in. Jesus **taught** his disciples. Is that rope **taut?** Don't **teaze** me. The river **Tees.** **Teas** have fallen in price. They **tracked** the thief through a large **tract** of marsh. Religious **Tract** Society. That man wanted **tact.** The squadron **tacked.** Income **tax.** **Tin-tacks.** The ship sailed on both **tacks.** **Two** sore **toes.** There is a steamer which **tows** **two** barges. You have **too** much **tow** in your pop-gun. A **ton** of coals. A **tun** of wine. The **toad** is a reptile. The ship was **towed** out of the river. A horse **tears** up the **tares** with his teeth. **Tare** is an allowance made on produce liable to waste. Don't **tear** me in pieces.

Exercise 59.

A **tear** bedews her eye. A box on the second **tier.** He was **thrown** from his horse. A sceptred monarch on his **throne.** I **told** you the bell **tolled** every **time** a person died. Wild **thyme.** He **throws** a stone. The death **throes** of the poor beast. The **tire** of a wheel. **Tyre** and Sidon. You **tire** me. She wore a **tiara** of diamonds. Bring up the supper **tray.** An unpleasant **trait** in his character. The peacock is a

vain bird. The jugular **vein.** A **vane** is a weather-cock. Rich **veins** of ore. **Vane** is a family name. In some sequestered **vale.** The lady wore a lace **veil.** The custom of giving **vails** at Christmas still **prevails.** The rising mist **unveils** a lovely scene.

Exercise 60.

The moon is on the **wane.** Charles' **wain,** or the Ceorl's **wain,** is a northern constellation. **Wait** till I know what the **weight** is. **Waste** not want not! A slender **waist.** A vast **waste** of country. The **way** was long. **Weigh** those **weys** of wool. Ducks **wade.** They **weighed** four pounds. A **weald** or wold is a forest. He knows how to **wield** a sword. **We'll** remain together in **weal** or woe. Are there any salmon **weirs** in the river **Wear?** What clothes do you **wear?** All sorts of **wares,** as earthenware, hardware, &c. **We're** all very **weary.** The mother will **wean** the child this **week.** A **weak** reply. To **ween** is to imagine. **Weights** and measures. The Christmas **waits.** **Would** you like to go into the **wood,** if the **weather** be fine? A **wether**-sheep. If we had a hoe, **we'd** soon **weed** the garden. **We've** just begun to **weave** the garlands. A high **wall.** Cats **waul.** A **wright** is a workman. Every body ought to read and **write.** **Wave** upon **wave** came rolling on the shore. Let us **waive** that point. The flag was **waving** in the breeze. **Waiving** that objection. The Prince of **Wales.** Loud **wails** and cries of woe. My **yoke** is easy. An egg with two **yolks.** Two **yokes** of oxen. Did **you** see the old **ewe** under the **yew** tree?

SECTION IV.

WORDS KINDRED IN SOUND, DISTINGUISHED BY A CORRECT
PRONUNCIATION, AND BY CONSIDERING THE
SENSE CONVEYED IN THEM.

Exercise 61.

The **altar** should not be **altered**. A horse **halter**.
He **affects** much, but **effects** little. They had **access**
to the library. **Excess** is always bad. The **Acts** of
the Apostles. A sharp **axe**. **Except** you **accede** to
my request and **accept** my **assistance**. They **exceed**
our desires. She lives **opposite**. An **apposite** remark. They had many **assistants**. Many **additions**
were made to the last **edition**. His **allusion** was a
complete **illusion**. He **alluded** to a matter which had
quite **eluded** my research. The **assay** office. He
wrote an **essay**. She was not **artless** but **heartless**.
Down in the **area** of that house. Esau was a **hairy**
man. The eagle's **eyry** was in rather an **airy**
position. What! are you **ailing**? It's **hailing** fast.
An **accessory** before the fact. They had every **accessary** possible. My **attendants** were rather lax in
their **attendance**. The Pretender's **adherents** gave
in their **adherence** to the Government. The mercer
was thoroughly **immersed**. The purser was **amerced** *
in a heavy fine. Bows and **arrows**. A **harrowing**
circumstance. A cool **arbour**. A **harbour** of refuge.
Ariel was a sprite. **Aerial** ways. **Aurora**, the goddess of morn. That horse was a **roarer**.

* A law term, = fined.

Exercise 62.

A **brood** of chickens. **Home-brewed** beer. He was **borne** to that **bourne** whence no traveller returns. **Bourne** or **burn** means a brook, as **Ravensbourne, Bannockburn.** An aider and **abetter** is little **better** than the actual thief. The **parlour-boarder** lost a handkerchief with a lace **border**. Great **benefits.** A rich **benefice.** The church **beadle.** A black **beetle.** Great **Britain.** A true **Briton.** **Barren** honour. The borough **borrowed** 1,000*l.* of the **baron.** Rabbits had **burrowed** in the old **barrow.** A **wheelbarrow.** The **baroness** deplored the **barrenness** of her land. The eyes of a **basilisk.** The **basilics,** or churches in Rome. **Close-fitting clothes.** In his **choler,** he took him by the **collar.** **Close** weather is bad for the **cholera.** Gold of 22 **carats.** A **caret** is a mark thus ∧. **Carrots** and parsnips. A Queen's **counsel.** The Privy **Council.** His **counsel** was good. That **cowherd** was an arrant **coward.** He **cowered** beneath my gaze. That person spent all his **salary** in **celery.** Two **copies** of the same book. A **coppice** of young oaks. They showed me great **courtesy.** The girl made a **curtsey.** The **courtesies** of life. Low **curtseys.**

Exercise 63.

Cease to do evil. **Seize** him. It was a clever **capture,** but the **captors** got nothing. Hymns and **chants.** By **chance** I saw your **cousin.** He tried to **cozen** me. That **critic** wrote a venomous **critique.** According to the **current** quotation, the price of **currants** has declined. **Cedars** of Lebanon. **Seceders** from the Union. That **leather-seller** lived in a **cellar.** That severe **censor censured** the minister for allowing **censers** in the church, and very **sensibly**

too. The Prince **Consort** gave a **concert**. They con-
certed the plan among themselves. The **counsellor**
said he should **commence** by making some **comments**
on the **correspondence** of the **co-respondents**. My
correspondents' letters were a **confirmation** of the
fact. A bad **conformation** of the body. The **Capitol**
at Rome. A **capital** offence. Great **symmetry** of
arrangement was observed in the **cemetery**. A
cocoa-nut. Chocolate is made from the **cacao** nut.
Chair. **Charwoman**. **Century**. **Sentry**. **Castor**
(beaver). **Caster**. **Cavalier**. **Caviller**. **Chagrin**.
Shagreen. **Calendar**. **Calender**. **Compliment**.
Complement. The **colander** is a **culinary** utensil.
The rude **Carinthian** boor. **Corinthian** columns.

Exercise 64.

A **dense** forest. **Dents** in a razor. **Divers** persons.
Diverse opinions. Two bucks and three **does**. That
dose of physic made him **doze**. I quite **dissent** from
you. Swift is the **descent** to evil. The **deceased**
had been **disseised*** of his property, and could
not therefore **devise** it. **Divisor** and **dividend**. Dis-
eased meat. With due **deference** to you, I don't see
the **difference**. His **dependants** were in a state of
abject **dependence**. After **dessert** the traveller **dis-
serted** on the fact of his having been **deserted** in the
desert. Somebody told him he had only got his
deserts. A **knight-errant**. That **errand** boy was an
arrant rogue. An **emigrant** from England is called
an **immigrant**, on arriving in America or Australia.
The Picts made many **irruptions** into England. Frequent **eruptions** of Vesuvius. That **eminent** person
was in **imminent** danger of losing his life. His
Eminence the Cardinal. The **imminence** of the

* Seised, disseised, and devise, are law terms.

danger did not deter him.   Can you elicit that fact
from him ?   An **illicit** still.

Exercise 65.

The **fool** was **full** of his nonsense.   The **fisherman**
sat in a **fissure** of the rock.   A **kingfisher**.   He was
formerly a cobbler.   I was received very **formally**.
In Egypt agriculturists are called **fellahs**.   That
gluttonous fellow liked everything **glutinous**.   What
a pretty **grot** !   Not worth a **groat**.   **Gristly** meat.
A **grizzly** bear.   **Grisly** spectres.   Avoid **gambling**.
The lambs were **gambolling** in the field.   The **gorilla**
is one of the largest species of monkeys.   **Guerillas**
are irregular troops, called so in Spain.   He shot a
heron.   As dead as a **herring**.   That **holy** man was
wholly dependent on charity.   His stockings were
holey.   To trundle a **hoop**.   The savages' **war-whoop**.
The **whooping-cough**.   It was a **hoax** which I **abhor**.
The sturdy **oaks**.   **Hoar** frost.   Pull the **oar**.   The
hussars waved their swords, and cried **huzza**.   The
hosier lost himself among the **osiers**.   Our **humble**
and **hearty** thanks.   You shall eat **umble*** pie.

Exercise 66.

What **gestures** did that **jester** make !   He was a
clever **juggler** ; for **instance**, he cut his **jugular** vein,
and was well again after a few **instants**.   Of course
he was an **impostor**, and his act a rank **imposture**.
To all **intents** and purposes.   **Intense** agony.   **Lower**
the boats !   Legendary **lore**.   An old **law**.   **Lower**
down the river.   I was very **loth** to do it.   I **loath**
the very sight of it.   What a **loathsome** spectacle !
David's tuneful **lute**.   **Loot** is plunder in war.   Don't
lose your **lesson**.   If you **loose** the rope, you will

* Umbles, the entrails of the deer.

lessen the strain. Along the **littoral** of the Mediterranean. A **literal** translation. They were **lightening** the ship. Thunder and **lightning**. Every member of the **legislature** ought to be a **legislator**. Spanish **licorice** (liquorice). **Lickerish** viands. Every **lineament** of his face was disfigured by the corrosive **liniment**. The **Jacobites** were the followers of James II.; the **Jacobins**, the extreme democratic faction during the French revolution.

Exercise 67.

The **miner's manner** was very abrupt. This **manor** belongs to a young man who is still a **minor.** The Israelites fed on **manna**. The **Moor** asked for **more.** Four **mowers** in the field. I am very fond of bread and **mustard**. The Israelites bred and **mustered**. A telegraphic **message**. All this **messuage** is to be let. **Mussels** are shell-fish. The **muzzle** of a dog. Bone and **muscle**. A **missile** is anything thrown. **Mizzling** rain. A Catholic **missal**. The **mistletoe**. Mice **gnaw**. The mutiny at the **Nore**. Otter-hunting is now rare in England. **Otto, ottar,** or **attar** of roses. He goes to consult the **oracle.** The left **auricle** of the heart. **Oracular** powers. **Auricular** confession. **Ordinances** have been often enforced by **ordnance.** He **pored** so long over the book that the perspiration **poured** from every **pore** down the **poor** fellow's face. **Plated** goods. **Plaited** straw. The **pastor's pastures** were very fertile. A statue of **Pallas** stood in the **palace** garden. A **prier** into other men's secrets. It was **prior** to that event. To **prescribe** medicine. To **proscribe** rebels.

Exercise 68.

Pontius **Pilate**. A **pilot**-boat. The **pillars** of Hercules. Downy **pillows**. His **presence** at Christ-

mas was always productive of many **presents**. **A**
bundle of **patterns**. A pair of **pattens** for dirty
weather. The **plaintiff** said in a **plaintive** tone, that
his **principal** aim was to uphold the **principle** of the
thing. A tall **poplar** tree. He was **popular** among
his fellows. That **prophet** has no **principle**, except
his own **profit**. When he **prophesies** in the most
populous parts, his **prophecies** are laughed at by the
populace. **Prepositions** do not connect **propositions**.
The **President**, by his **proscriptions** of the chief
men, set a bad **precedent**. **Patients** should practise
patience by learning to read their physicians' **pre-
scriptions**. A **parricide**. Every animal has its
peculiar **parasite.**

Exercise 69.

He **roars** with pain. The **rowers** were worn out
by fatigue. This meat is **rawer** than that. A **rude**
and illiterate man. A **rood** is the fourth part of an
acre. He **rued** the day for all his life. A clever
ruse. She **rues** that deed. A **reel** of cotton. **Real**
pleasure. The Highland **reel.** Some **radishes** are
reddish, others white. The **regiment** was put under
strict **regimen** during the epidemic. Among his
relics was an old **razor**. A widow is often called
the **relict** of her husband. A fine **racer.** An **inky**
razor. An **ink-eraser.** The extreme **rigour** of the
law. Wanted some good **riggers** in the dockyard.
Rime frost. Without **rhyme** or reason. There is no
room here. He has a **rheum.** Covered with **ridicule.**
A lady's **reticule.** Among the **residents** of the place.
This delightful **residence** to be let. The **rabbit** is
very prolific. **Rabbet** is a term in carpentry.

Exercise 70.

Sword in hand. On the green **sward.** His
imagination **soared** too high. The fair **sex.** Many

religious **sects.** **Succour** the poor and needy. The
suckers of a plant. The **satires** of Horace. Fauns and
satyrs. **Symbols** are signs. **Cymbals** are musical in-
struments. The hill of **Sion.** **Scion** of a noble house.
As the boat was a bad **sailer,** and he a worse **sailor,**
it was a **silly** thing to cross over to the **Scilly** Islands.
The **sculptor** had a **spacious** room for his **statues** and
other **sculpture.** Thy **statutes** are right. A **specious**
argument. Dissenters object to the **surplice.** He
had a **surplus** of money in hand. **Sanitary** measures.
A **sanatory** establishment. Are you his **senior?**
Signor is the Italian, **Sènor** the Spanish, for Sir. The
Sultan of Turkey is the grand **Seignior.**

Exercise 71.

He **threw** a stone **through** the window. The
present **tense** or time. To your **tents,** Oh Israel!
Use your **talents** profitably. The eagle took up the
lamb in its **talons.** Are you going to **travel?** He
shall see of the **travail** of his soul and be satisfied.
Several **treaties** have been signed in Paris. He
wrote a **treatise** about them. A **tenor** singer. Preserve the even **tenour** of your way. His **tenure** of
that property was open to objection.

N.B.—Wh. *h* should be aspirated.

Brilliant **verdure.** A **verger** in the Cathedral. A
dreary **way.** Curds and **whey.** The wool **weighs**
three **weys.** **Where** were your **wares** placed? I
cannot come upon you **unawares**; you are too **wary.**
What clothes did **Wat** Tyler **wear?** He **wore** a leather
jacket. In peace or **war** I have your **word.** A **ward**
in Chancery. **Wardrobe** is the French garde-robe.
In **weal** or **woe** we'll stand by you. A carter says
whoa! to his horses. The **weald** of Kent. The
regiment **wheeled** to the right. **Wield** not the sword
in vain.

Exercise 72.

Our **world** continually **whirls** round. Don't **whine** in that manner. That is **vile wine**. A sharp **file**. A bass **viol**. A **vial** or **phial** of vitriol. **Venus**, the goddess of beauty. **Venous** blood. The **valleys** of the **Valais** in Switzerland. That gentleman's **valet** lost his master's **valise**. **Whether** the **weather** be **wet** or not, we must look after the lost **wether**. The boar **whets** his tusks. Your **wit** is not a **whit** better than mine. A **witling** is a man of little wit. Some Americans have a habit of **whittling** a stick, or even the leg of the table. **Whither** are you going ? The flowers begin to **wither**. Are you a **whig** ? Wait **while** I put on my **wig**. **Wile** away the time with **what** you can. **Wot** ye not that it was I? **Wat** is the familiar name for Walter. **Which** do you prefer ? Wizard and **witch** have the same derivation. The **whaler bewails** his hard fate, at having taken only 100 **whales**. He was very **wicked**. The Prince of **Wales** knocked the bails off the **wicket**. In days of **yore**. You're quite sure you have **your** own **ewer**, are you? **Whitebait** and **whiting** are fishes. **Whitening** is prepared chalk. What an unlucky **wight** ! The Isle of **Wight**.

SECTION V.

WORDS SPELT EXACTLY ALIKE, THE SOUND OF WHICH IS
VARIED BY ACCENT, AS CÓNSORT, CONSÓRT.

Exercise 73.

Nouns and adjectives have the accent on the first,
verbs on the last syllable, in dissyllables, and the
last but one in trisyllables.

The **convict** has been thrice **convicted**. That
contract is null and void. He **contracts** by the year.
I **conjure** you do not **conjure** in my presence. What
a **contrast**! Do not **contrast** them too closely.
Hallam **records** that event; he took it from the state
records. A **transfer** of the property. **Transfer** your
claim to me. The ordnance **survey**. I'm monarch
of all I **survey**. The murderer was **respited**, but the
respite came too late. Moral **attributes**. Do you
attribute that to me? The **incense** floating in the
air. Don't **incense** me.

Exercise 74.

Words in *se*, spelt alike, but varied by the *z* sound
in verbs, as use, *v.*, use, *n.*

Abuse is bad, so never **abuse** any person or thing.
Excuse me, I will take no **excuse**. **Grease** the wheels
with tallow **grease**. A fine **house**. The corn is all
housed. Do not **close** the door this **close** weather.
His style was **diffuse**, yet the whole book was **dif-
fused** with irony. Don't **chastise** him, much as he
deserves **chastisement.**

E

Exercise 75.

In many words the verb is written with *z* or *s*, and the noun with *c*.

Practice makes perfect, so **practise** much and often. He **devises** new schemes, but his **devices** seldom succeed. **Devices** on a shield. He **devised** his property among his kindred. To **prize** anything is to set a high **price** upon it. They **chased** the stag. Chevy **Chace.** The plate was richly **chased.** Unbounded **licence.** To **license** printing. That **licensed victualler** had two **licences. Practising** on the piano. Eschew evil **practices.***

* The spelling of *c* for the noun and *s* for the verb is very irregular with English writers. In the Game Licences issued in 1866, *licence* and *license* were both written as the noun. Webster has *practice, licence,* both noun and verb.

SECTION VI.

Double Consonants.

Bb, cc, dd, ff, gg, ll, mm, nn, pp, rr, ss, tt, zz.
N.B.—*V* is never found doubled.
N.B.—Monosyllables seldom end in a single *f, s, l,* or *z.*
The exceptions are, *as, us, has, gas, this, thus, if, of, yes, quiz,* &c.
A single *s* seldom ends any word, except as the inflexion of nouns and verbs, and in the following: *alas! bias, canvas* (coarse cloth), *omnibus,* &c., and the compounds of *mass,* as *Christmas.*

Exercise 76.

Ebb tide. New-laid eggs. An ell of cloth. Doff your hat. Banns of marriage. You err greatly. Cats purr. The ass liked chaff. The tall lass had a doll in her muff. He lolls at the inn door. The bell tolls for mass. Bees buzz. Bullets whizz. Serpents hiss. A gruff voice. Two butts of sherry. Bulls butt with their horns. Lloyd is a Welsh name.
Exception. Coal gas.

Exercise 77.

A cobbler's stall. He drew the sword, and threw away the scabbard. A rapid eddy. The dog's kennel. Gibbet and gallows. It puzzles me why you giggle. A carrion crow. Cabbages and carrots. The caitiff wore handcuffs. A grizzly bear. The gizzard of a buzzard. A haggard face. Immense traffic. Drizzling rain. The sheriff had a warrant.

Can you **suggest** a cure for the **hiccoughs?** A **stirrup** cup. His name is in the **gazette.** What a ʻcoquette!

N.B.—A strong **bias.** His mind was **biassed.** A **canvas** tent. Did you **canvass** for votes? **Alas!** poor Yorick! **Christmas** day.

cribbage, doggrel, flaccid, mammon, dizzy, tariff, plaintiff, balloon, cesspool, proffer, scraggy, allure, puzzle, corvette, assess, harass, ellipse.

Exercise 78.

A strong **garrison.** The **assassin** of the President. The **Apennines** swarm with **banditti. Chiccory** in the coffee. The **attorneys** and **barristers exaggerated** the **business.** A **robbery** was **committed** in the **shrubbery** adjoining the **nunnery.** He **embezzled** money. **Paraffin** oil. A **colossal** statue stood in the **colonnade.** The **assailants** were **stopped** by a **barricade. Llewellyn** is a Welsh name. **Ammonia effervesces** with acids.

essential, cannibal, satellite, allegory, assaulted, saccharine, eccentricities, Michaelmas, scurrilous, coquetting, gazetted, garotted, pusillanimity, harass, embarrass, tyrannize, inflammable, philippics.

Further examples of double consonants are given in that section treating on prefixes and affixes.

Exercise 79.

The student is apt to be often misled by the accent, or by ignorance of the derivation, to double the consonant in the middle of words. The following exercises of mixed words are therefore added for practice.

He **announced** his presence **annually** by sending an **anonymous** letter. **Anointed** king. An **immense** amount of **ammunition.** A comma is a short pause.

Did you see the **comet**? Three **copies**. Opium is extracted from **poppies**. The **coppice** was full of game. An eagle's **talons**. **Tallow** candles. A man of **talent**, but a great **bigot**. Full of **maggots**. Throw **faggots** on the fire. Put the **spigot** in the cask. The knight took the **dragon** away in a **waggon**. A **flagon** of ale. **Coral** Islands. **Sorrel** is a herb with a sour taste. A **placid** countenance. **Flaccid** muscles. The **rabbit** became **rabid**. His face was **pallid**, and his appearance **squalid** in the extreme. A **florid** complexion. The **torrid** zone was **horridly** hot.

Exercise 80.

A **valid** objection. **Stolid** qualities. His **pallor** did not affect his **valor**. Be **merry** and wise. **Merit** always finds the day. He kept a **ferret**. **Malice** is to be reproved. The **trellis** work in the garden. He hit her with a **mallet**. The **palate** of the mouth. **Melons** cannot be too **mellow**. A **felon's** garb. **Melodious** and **mellifluous** sounds. A dish of **salad**. What a pretty **ballad**. As he lay that night on his **pallet** of straw. Vote by **ballot**. An unjust **balance** is an abomination. His **banner** hung over the **balusters** or **banisters**. A **canister** of tea. Those men are **cannibals**. The town was full of **alleys**. **Lilies** of the **valley**. A **linen** shirt. The **linnet** sang sweetly. **Syrup** of roses. Hold the **stirrup** while I mount. He **proffered** something that was much **preferable**.

Exercise 81.

The **pommel** of a saddle. **Pumice** stone. **Medlars** are eaten when rotten. The **peddler** came once a year. The **minions** of Edward II. Are you fishing with a **minnow**? Under the **shadow** of a sycamore tree. **Madder** is a dye. Simon the **tanner**. A splendid **manor**. A **million** of facts. The **pavilion** at Brighton. What a smart **postillion**! **Vermilion** is a compound of mercury. The guard was **patrolled** every morning. All the **militia** officers were **paroled**. That **querulous** fellow was always **quarrelling**. **Elastic** bands. Its form was **elliptical**. That **colloquy** took place in the **Coliseum**. He had great **ability**. A scene of **tranquillity**. **Harassed** by many **embarrassments**.

Exercise 82.

The **wizard** had a tame **lizard**. His writings were **scurrilous** and **libellous**. Such **perilous** adventures are quite **marvellous**. His agony was **aggravated** by the treatment. **Enveloped** in mystery. **Undeveloped** resources. He was not **eligible**, because his writing was **illegible**. Did you **relish** your dinner? The book was **embellished** with engravings. Jupiter's **satellites**. His **salary** was 10*l*. a year. A picture **gallery**. **Capillary** attraction. The **abolition** of the slave trade. An **ebullition** of temper. **Vaccination** modifies small-pox. **Vacillating** conduct. He feigned **imbecility**. Such **superciliousness** was only a mark of **pusillanimity**. **Britannia** needs no bulwarks. The bank was full of **bullion**. **Bulrushes**. The dukes of **Brittany**. Rule **Britannia**.* Are you a **teetotaller**? **Teetotalism**. **Philip**. Port **Phillip**.† The **Philippics** of Demosthenes.

* Brittannia, thus spelt on the coinage of George III.

† Port Phillip in Australia, always so spelt in home and colonial papers.

SECTION VII.

Mute Consonants, and Consonants having Varying Sounds.

b mute, as *dumb, subtle.*

c mute, as *victuals,* and in all SYLLABLES where *c* follows *s,* and precedes *k.*

ch mute, in *schism, yacht.*

d semi-mute, as *handsome.*

g mute before *n,* as *gnat, deign.*

gh is always mute in the middle of a simple word.

h mute in the beginning of many words, such as *heir,* and in all foreign words.

In words beginning with *gh, rh, wh,* the *h* should be aspirated.

k mute before *n,* as *know, knob.*

l mute, as *palm, half, Lincoln.*

m mute, as in *mnemonics.*

n mute, as *hymn, damn.*

p mute, as *receipt, symptom.*

s mute, as *isle, demesne.*

w mute, when following *m, n, l, r* in proper names, as *Harwich, Greenwich, Lerwick ;* when before *r* the *r* should be slightly rolled, as *wren.*

Lastly, it should be remembered that, in all French words not naturalised, the final consonant is not sounded, as *chamois.*

Exercise 83.

The **plumber** was deaf and **dumb**. **Crumbs** of bread. **Pumpkin**-pie. The licensed **victualler** was **indicted** at the assizes. That **haughty** peer was

arraigned for treason, and sentenced to condign
punishment. A schism in the church. You will not
impugn my authority with impunity. He gnashed
his teeth. The mouse gnawed the lion's net. A
gnarled oak. His chest was loaded with phlegm.
Six weeks' furlough. The handsomest man in
Brighton. A beautiful vignette. The knell of
parting day. A knobby stick. A knotty question.
The men put off their knapsacks and bivouacked on
a shady knoll. The Lord High Almoner distributed
alms. We went deer stalking, but were balked of
our sport. Malmsey wine. Psalms and hymns, and
solemn songs. Pneumatics is the science of aërial
bodies.

Exercise 84.

The abbot had many sumpter mules. He jambed
his thumb and grazed his knuckles, when alighting
from the sleigh. Raspberry jam. The qualms of
conscience produce poignant anguish. A puisne
judge. The viscount gave a receipt for the champagne. The campaigns of Marlborough. Do you
live at Harwich or Woolwich? I did live at Lincoln,
but have removed to Norwich.

dough, drought, knead, Isle of Wight, balmy,
feign, salmon, malign, chalk, aisle, gnat, yacht,
slough, gherkin, salve, borough, freighted, half-pence,
raspberries, consumption, presumption, &c., demesne,
chamois, peremptory, rendezvous, mnemonics, Warwick, Greenwich, Lerwick, &c.

Exercise 85.

The letter *s* having the sound of both *s* and *z*;
and *c* before *e, i, y*, having the sound of *s*, causes
frequent mistakes in spelling. The following sentences are added for practice.

With every course a different sauce. The very

essence of common **sense**. Cups and **saucers**. **Hawsers** are thick ropes used on board ships. She looked from the **lattice pensively**. The **trellis** work cost only a few **pence**. The line was **traced** and then **erased**. Some **terse** remarks were made at the **rehearsal**. A **dervise** lived in that **crevice** in the rock. Do not **coerce** him. **Disperse** the mob. The elective **franchise**. All the **novices** on the **premises** wore **surplices**. **Rinse** that **chalice**. A pair of **pincers**. **Ancient** friends. **Transient** pleasures. He had **exquisite** manners. **Incite** not to evil. A very **apposite** and **explicit** remark. The **perquisites** were divided among the servants.

Exercise 86.

The **missiles** penetrated his **domicile**. **Pacify** that poor child! Can you not **classify** those subjects? The judges on **circuit** dined off a **sirloin** of beef. On the top of the **cenotaph** was a **seraph**. An attack of **jaundice**. **Pumice** stone. An **armistice** for three months was concluded. His **taciturnity** was very **asinine**. The army was **decimated**, and the dead were interred in the **cemetery**. A **seminary** is a place to **disseminate** learning. **Supercilious** behaviour. **Oscillating** engines. **Acetic** acid. An **ascetic** monk.

Exercise 87.

ch has three sounds :—

ch = *k* in words derived from the Greek, as *chronic*.

ch = *tch*, *dsh* in Saxon words, as *Charles*.

ch = *sh* in French words, as *chamois*.

ch is mute in a few words, as *yacht*, *drachm*.

A shrill **echo**. The **yacht** anchored in the **channel**. **Charles** was of a **churlish character**. A large **catch** of **anchovies**. His **chilblains** ached. **Etchings** from nature. The **anchorite** saw a **chamois**. **Charlotte** died of **chagrin**. **Chancellor** of the **Exchequer**. **Chyme** and **chyle** are formed in digesting food. **Spinach** is a vegetable. An **ostrich's** egg. **Chalybeate** waters. The **chrysalis** of a butterfly. The **fuchsia** is so called from Fuchs, a German botanist.

chasm, chisel, distich, chariot, chaos, archdeacon, Michael, archangel, ochre, cherub, strychnine, chorister, chronicle, charivari, schismatic, crotchety, chloroform, chronometer, galoches.

Exercise 88.

sc, sch (*c, ch* mute), in words of classic derivation.

He wields the **sceptre**. A sharp **scythe**. The **scion** of a noble house. A **schism** in the church. He opened the **abscess** with a pair of **scissors**. God is **prescient** and **omniscient**. A **schedule** of his debts. The parties **coalesced**. A pleasant **reminiscence**. The **Scythians** wore **scimitars**. **Effervescing** draughts.

rescind, obscene, conscious, quiescent, scientific, excrescence, convalescent, scintillation, sciatica, fascinating.

Exercise 89.

sc = *sk*, chiefly in words of Saxon and Danish derivation.

squ = *skw*.

The boy **scrambled** through the thorns, and **scratched** his hands. The **scullion** was **scolded** for **scalding** himself while **scouring** out the **scullery**. A **skull** and a **skeleton**. The owl **screeches**. Pigs **squeak**. The **skipper** **squandered** his money at **skittles**. The **scavenger** stole the coal **scuttle** and **scrubbing** brush. The weather was too **squally** for the **squadron** to **skirmish**. **Scraggy** meat. A lively **squirrel**. Her face was so **scorched** and **scarred** that it quite **scared** me. The **scribe** was **scourged** for **scribbling scourrilous** and **scandalous** libels. He escaped **unscathed**.

scheme, scate, disc, scout, skilful, squeamish, skimmed, scutage, skewer, skating, scrawling, squatter, obelisk, scrutiny, microscopic, Isle of Skye, Schiedam.

Exercise 90.

Th in Saxon words has two sounds, as in *thin* and *thine*.

th = Greek θ (pronounced as *th* in *thin*).

th, h mute in *thyme, Thompson,* and in most French and German words.

The **thistles** were **thick** and **thriving** in his garden. Wild **thyme**. Bound with **withies**. **Blythe** as a lark. **Thirty-three themes** were read in the **theatre**. **Clothe** the naked. What is the **breadth** of the **isthmus** of Suez? It was quite a **myth**. **Orthography** and **orthoepy**. Yorkshire has **three trithings** or **ridings**. An attack of **asthma**.

writhe, rhythm, thrill, enthral, thorough, seething, athlete, lithograph, logarithm.

Exercise 91.

wh = *hw* A.-Saxon. *h* aspirated by public speakers.

A queer **whim**. Don't **whine** when you speak. Not a **whit** the better. The boar **whets** his tusks. The **wherry** was moored to the **wharf**. Never **whisper** in company. The **whooping** cough. The balls **whizzed** by his head. **Whig** and **whisky** are both Celtic words.

whist, whack, whirl, whelp, wheedle, whitlow, whistle, overwhelm, whittle, wheezing, whetstone, whimsical, whortleberry.

Exercise 92.

rh = Greek ῥ (aspirated).

Rhyme is distinct from **rhythm**. He had a **rheum** and the **rheumatics** at the same time. **Rhubarb** pills. Tincture of **myrrh**. You have a **catarrh** or cold in the head. A **rhombus** and a **rhomboid**. Homer's poems are called **rhapsodies**, but the meaning of the word is changed. **Rhetoric** is the art of speaking. The **rhinoceros** trampled down the **rhododendrons**. A **hæmorrhage** from the nose. An attack of **diarrhœa**. **Pyrrhus** was king of Epirus.

Exercise 93.

ph = *f* = Greek φ.

In many words the *ph* is written as well as pronounced *f*.

A **nymph** with a **sylph**-like form. A **phial** of **physic**. **Phases** or changes of the moon. **Typhus** fever. An **epitaph** on an **orphan** boy. The **physician** wrote a **graphic pamphlet** on **ophthalmic** diseases. His **philosophy** was mere **sophistry**. The **apocrypha**. The **apophthegms** of Bacon. **Phthisis** is a pulmonary disorder. **Pheasant** is from the French '**faisan**.'

lymph, sphynx, sphere, phalanx, hyphen, phantom, sulphur, sapphire, phrensy, philtre, caliph, naphtha, spherical, Pharisee, phosphorus, blasphemy, atmosphere, phlegmatic, catastrophe, euphony, geography, &c.; all words beginning with amphi, as amphibious.

Exercise 94.

wr is slightly rolled in the pronunciation by good speakers.

Wry faces. A **wreath** of roses. The worm **wriggled** and **writhed**. He **wrought** a good work.

First **wrangler**. A pretty **wren**. In his **wrath** he **wrenched** it from me and sprained my **wrist**. A **wrinkled** forehead. **Wrack** and ruin.

wreathe, wreak, wrung, wrapper.

ps = Greek ψ, is found in only a few words the *p* should be sounded.

Psyche (psike), **pshaw, psalmody, psychology, apocalypse.**

SECTION VIII.

On the Composition of Words.

The simplest form of a word is called its *root*.

A syllable put before the root is called a *prefix*.

A syllable put after the root is called an *affix* or *suffix*.

The prefixes and affixes are either Saxon, Latin, or Greek.

The spelling of the root word is often varied by these prefixes and affixes, as the following Exercises will show.

Most of the prefixes and affixes are pronounced as written. Many of the *prefixes*, however, undergo a change in their final consonant, for the sake of euphony: for example, with the Latin and Greek prefixes, *ad*, *con* (*co*), *in*, *e* (*ex*), *ob*, *sub*, *syn*, the final consonant generally becomes the same as the initial consonant of the root word, as *affix*, *aggrieve*, *correspond*, *illegal*, *immutable*, *effusion*, *occur*, *suffuse*, *syllable*, *symmetry*. The exceptions are, however, numerous.

N.B.—In the spelling of words in which the final letter of the prefix and the initial letter of the affix are the same as the initial or final letter of the root, care must be taken not to drop one of the consonants. See Ex. 102. The confusion of the sound of the prefixes *in* and *e* in such words as *immigrant*, *emigrant*, *imminent*, *eminent*, &c.; as also of *pre* and *pro*, *ante*, *anti*, in *prescribe*, *proscribe*, *anteroom*, *antidote*, &c., must be guarded against, by considering the sense conveyed in the word. Examples have already been given in Section IV.

As the greatest irregularity exists in the spelling of many derivative * words in English, the following rules are intended only as guides to the student as to the manner in which such words are spelt by the best writers of his day.

N.B.—It should be remarked, that English writers will *not* follow Webster in his spelling of compound words.

Exercise 95.

The *e* final of root words is dropped before affixes beginning with a vowel, except the sound of the consonant preceding the *e* is damaged thereby. This is found to be the case after *g* † and *c* (soft), and sometimes *k, v, m, l, t.*‡

When the *e* is part of a written diphthong in a monosyllable, it is preserved before *ing*, as *hoeing, shoeing, eyeing, iceing, seeing, fleeing,* &c. ; except *ie*, as *vie, vying* ; or when *ed, er* follow *ee*, as *freer, fee'd,* &c. ; and in a few other words, as *truism, bluish.*

Seeing is **believing**. After **dyeing** the stuff, it was **unsalable**. He was of a **lovable** and amiable disposition. A **notable** character. The **statuary** was **irretrievably** lost. **Movable** property is not **ratable**. The **icy** pole. **Juicy** meat. A **rosy** hue. **Stony** roads. A **marriageable** girl. His legs were **twinge-**

---

* The pupil should have explained to him the distinction between a *derived* and a *compound* word. A derivative consists of *one* root-word, having either an affix or a prefix common to whole classes of words, as *blackish, bluish.* A compound word is the union of *two* or more distinct roots, as *shoe-black, sky-blue.*

† Except when *g = dg*, as *alleging.*

‡ Loveable, moveable, tameable, saleable, rateable, irreconcileable, unmistakeable, &c., now generally spelt without the *e.*

ing with **aguish** symptoms. **Changeableness** of the weather. The hyæna is said to be **untamable**. A **gluey** substance. The blood **tingeing** the river was **traceable** for a long distance. One man was **hoeing** potatoes, the other was occupied in **shoeing** and **singeing** an **unmanageable** horse. They were **iceing** the wine. He was **eyeing** the proceedings with a **roguish** smile. **Alleging** what was not true, and **pledging** his honour thereto, he **sacrilegiously** * perjured himself. **Irreconcilable** to his principles.

whitish, sueing, cooing, cooed, wooed, truism, fringeing, hingeing, mileage, acreage, seizable, grievous, haranguing, rescuing, ruing, accruing, &c. ; unmistakably, changeable, chargeable, serviceable, damageable, chastity, orangeade, noticing, noticeable, unpalatable, enticing, enticeable, advantageous, courageous, &c. ; whereunto, thereabouts, hereupon.

Exercise 96.

The *e* final is preserved before affixes beginning with a consonant, except after the sound *dg* ; or after *e* when it is part of a written diphthong, as *truly*, *awful* also in the word *wholly*.

That **advertisement** was a shameful **infringement** on **politeness**, and merited a **wholesome chastisement**. God's **judgments** are slow, but **surely** just. He came to an **arrangement** and gave an **acknowledgment**. His **movements** were **awfully** slow. His sad **bereavement** caused a **derangement** of the intellect. An **abridgment** of Macaulay's History. The troops **duly** effected a **lodgment** in the citadel.

solely, woful, ceaseless, hoarseness, forehead, guileless, looseness, achievement, chasteless.

* The *e* in such words as *sacrilege* becomes *i* before *ous.*

Exercise 97.

On doubling the final consonant.

All monosyllables ending in a single consonant which is preceded by a single vowel, double invariably their final consonant, with an affix, commencing with a vowel, as *glad, gladden.*

He **shunned** society. The fire has been **stirred. Shamming** illness. A boar **whetting** his tusks. He was always **quizzing** his friend. The swallow **wagged** his tail, and **flapped** his wings. **Charred** wood. **Wrapped** in a **reddish**-looking cloak. **Skimmed** milk. **Throbbing** temples. The **druggist,** after having been **stabbed,** was **dragged** into a ditch. A **craggy** place. The **starry** heavens. A **tarry** jacket. Fierce **warriors.** A **robbery** was committed in the **shrubbery.** She went into a **nunnery. Barristers** like briefs.

Exceptions to this established rule of our language seem to occur in the words *manikin, panikin.*

Words of more than one syllable, ending in a single consonant, preceded by a single vowel (sometimes a diphthong, *equalled, equipped*), double the final consonant with affixes beginning with a vowel *only* when the accent falls on the last syllable, as *begin-ning, transfer-red.*

Exceptions : most words ending in *l,* and the compounds of *worship* ; as *worshipper, worshipped.*

All verbs ending in *l,** having affixes *ed, ing, er,* double the *l,* with the exception of *unparalleled.*

---

* The letter *l* is the despair of schoolboys. Webster makes the doubling of this letter conform to the rule, as also do many of the makers of spelling-books, but English writers will not follow it. The one exception 'unparalleled' is the only persistent instance of the *l* not being doubled that I have been able to remark, during the last three or four years, in the ' Times' and

Exercise 98.

In words ending in *l* with other affixes, such as *ous, ist, ize, ity,* &c., the doubling of the *l* cannot be brought to any rule. The derivation of the word is the best guide. Compare *novelist, duellist, pugilist; perilous, marvellous; civility, tranquillity; equalize, tranquillize;* note also *imbecile, imbecility; inflame, inflammable; tyrant, tyrannise; Philip, Philippics; epigram, epigrammatical.*

N.B.—Beware of doubling the letter *t,* in such words as *riveting, carpeted, benefited, fidgety, maggoty, bonneted, crotchety,* &c.; let their spelling follow the rule *not* to double the final consonant, except the accent falls on the last syllable of the simple word.

Though **differing** from him, he still, with due **deference, preferred** his own opinion to that of the **barrister,** who **offered** him **excellent** advice. He was an aider and **abettor** in those **libellous** proceedings. **Carolling** light as lark at morn. One regiment, fully **equipped,** was **picketed** outside the town, another was **billeted** on the inhabitants. The church was thronged with **worshippers,** when an **appalling** accident **imperilled** their lives. **Gossiping** about

leading writers of the day. In many of these words given for example, as *chiselled* (Fr. *ciselé*), the *l* ought, according to the derivation of the word, undoubtedly not to be doubled. Yet the nature of that letter is so liquid, that it is almost invariably doubled, in spite of Walker, Webster, and all who frame their spelling on those models. What with the doubt about doubling the *l* in some words, and dropping it in others (in such a class of words as *recal*), schoolboys are thoroughly perplexed. 'How will the examiners mark us?' say they. 'If we spell REVELLING with one *l*, and DOWNFAL with two; shall we lose our marks?' And their perplexity, poor boys, must remain, until it please the literary and learned men of England to form themselves into an academy, and settle English spelling by their authority. Till then, there must be a sort of free trade in orthography.

trifles. He **galoped** furiously along. That **pugilist** was a noted **duellist**. The **jeweller** sold me an **enamelled medallion**. He **benefited** mankind as **befitted** his station in life. They **proffered** their aid, which **profited** little.

Exercise 99.

A double-**barrelled** gun. Always see your luggage **labelled**. A newly **carpeted** room. That **novelist** was **unrivalled** in his **raillery**. Such **tyrannical** proceedings were **unparalleled**. **Crystalline** waters. **Coralline** islands. The **Sybilline** books. A plot of land was **allotted** to the licensed **victualler**. A **rickety** table. A **rackety** fellow. Gorgeously **apparelled**. The **civilian's acquittal** was sure. The Alps are being **tunnelled**. Old china **riveted** here. An **unbiassed** opinion. The **levellers** were the extreme party in the so called Great **Rebellion**. Many of the wounded were **bayoneted. Shivering** with cold. **Quivering** with rage. The **distiller annulled** the bargain, and **cancelled** the agreement. A **crotchety** old fellow was in a state of **imbecility. Carbureted** gases.

Exercise 100.

differed, transferred, beginner, bigoted, debarred, propeller, coveted, tranquillity, equalize, abhorred, gambolling, jewellery (jewelry), perilous, pommelled, unequalled, equality, marvellous, marshalled, patrolled, paroled, enveloped, developed, unlimited, japanned, unkennelled, cricketers, caviller, pocketed, regretted, ticketed, acquitted, chiselled, vomited, woollen, realize, bonneted, preferring, groveller, quarrelling, inflammable, neutralize, wainscoting, velvety, committed, merited, filliped, Philippics, pencillings, impannelled, balloted, combating, modeller, piloted, gravelly, closeted, cudgelled, gibbeted, curveted, dieted, quieted, kidnapping, ricocheted, spavined.

Exercise 101.

On dropping the final *l* of simple words in composition.

RULE.—*All* and *full* always drop one *l*, as *although, awful*, except in compound words separated by a hyphen, as *all-seeing, full-grown*.

In all other words ending in *ll*, the contradictions of dictionary makers, correctors for the press, and our best writers, are so numerous, that nothing like a rule can be laid down.

It may, however, be remarked, that words ending in *ll* always drop one *l* before the affixes *less* and *ly*, as *skilless, dully*.

Also, that there is a tendency among English (not American) writers to drop one *l*, with some affixes and prefixes in many words, such as *dulness, downfal, recal, enrol, distil.**

The spelling here given is that which seems to predominate among English writers.

Almost, withal, almighty, all-seeing, awful, albeit, fulfil, skilful, skilless, fulsome, bashful, &c.; wilful, fullness, full-dressed, unwell, welcome, farewell, welfare, stillness, dullness, smallness, tallness, bulldog, bulrush, bulwark, bellman, millstone, downfall, appal, enthral, thraldom, forestall, foretell, refill, undersell, enrol, repel, distil, befall, befell, waterfall, chilblain, shrillness, still-born, rebel, dispel.†

---

* Perhaps the safer plan for the student to adopt, in the spelling of all these disputed words, is, to write them with two *ll*'s, excepting words with *all* and *full*, and a few other familiar ones, such as *welfare, skilful, until, wilful, bulrush, fulfil*, &c.

† Note that all these words which drop the *l* take it again in composition with other affixes, as *rebel-led, dispel-ling*.

Exercise 102.

In the spelling of compound words, in which the final letter of the prefix and the initial letter of the root, and the final letter of the root and the first letter of the affix, are the same, care must be taken not to drop one of the consonants.

N.B.—In the spelling of all compound words having prefixes and affixes, the pupil should be taught to pull the word to pieces, and, having arrived at the root, to build the word up again, first by adding the prefix, then the affix, or *vice versâ*.

He **connived** at the other's fault. They felt **aggrieved**. When **immured** in a dungeon, he saw an **appalling apparition**. Never **misspend** your time. A **soulless** man. **Genteelly apparelled**. The **commissary** was **dissatisfied**, and **dissuaded** his colleague. The **barrenness** of the land was **irremediable**. Railway **collisions** were of frequent **occurrence**. The **suddenness** of the attack alarmed him. Perfect **symmetry** of form. Great **openness** of manner was combined with **eccentricity**. The country was **overrun** with **immigrants**. Those **innovations** were **illegally** carried out.

occult, apprize, arraign, illiterate, syllogism, evenness, illicit, effervesce, dissimilar, dissolute, elliptical, allegory, dissension, appraised, annihilated, aggrandisement, irreproachable, acclimatisation, immured, illegible.

SECTION IX.

DIFFICULT AND PUZZLING TERMINATIONS.

Exercise 103.

The spelling of words ending in *le* must be distinguished from that of words having the same, or nearly the same sound, ending in *al, el, il, ol, ul, yl*. Compare *apple, chapel; mettle, metal; spittle, Spitalfields*.

The lamb **gambols** around the **shambles**. Take away that **bauble**. The **thimble** is the **symbol** of woman's industry. A **fickle** person. The Jewish **shekel** and the Chinese **picul** are weights. It was a **miracle** he did not cut himself with the **sickle**. Are you fond of **pickle**? **Nickel** is a metal. **Manacles** are handcuffs. A **clerical chronicle**. The **critical** moment arrived. A **cycle** of years. A pair of **spectacles**. **Technical** errors. **Feudal** times. A new **mangle**. The **bridal** party offered a **medal** for the best **riddle**. The **caudal** appendage of a French **poodle**. An iron **kettle**. The **petals** of a flower. He was **muffled** in furs. **Shuffle** the cards. The **vulture** feeds on **offal**. **Doggrel** verses. A stout **cudgel**. The **panel** of a jury. Coarse **flannel**. **Carnal** lusts. A **charnel** house. The **Sibyl** had a **subtle** manner. **Apostle**. **Vertical**.

Exercise 104.

The **Gospel** was read in the **chapel**. Three **scruples** make one drachm. A **barrel** of **mussels**. **Pencils** and **chisels**. A school-boy's **sachel**. Christmas **carols**. Salts of **sorrel**. **Coral** beads. He had a **tassel** to his cap. **Tinsel** is very evanescent. The **mistral** is called a N.E. wind in the Mediterranean. Put that **whistle** on the **mantel** piece. The **teasel** is a kind of **thistle**. A shoal of **mackerel**. The **beryl** is a **jewel**. Catch a **weasel** asleép. The biscuit was full of **weevils**. An attack of **measles**. **Shrivelled myrtles**. A **swivel** gun. They put gorgeous **apparel** on the **prodigal** son. A heavy **vehicle**. A **metrical** romance. The **perusal** of his **epistle** took some time. What a gay **carnival**! The **citadel** surrendered. There was not a **particle** of truth in that **scandal**. **Spherical** trigonometry.

recital, oracle, nostril, tonsil, cuticle, reciprocal, &c.

Exercise 105.

Words ending in *cy*, *sy*, with their inflexions in *cies*, *sies*.

Cy comes mostly from French words in *nce*, as *excellency*.

Sy from the Greek or Latin, as *ecstasy*.

Sound **policy**. An attack of **pleurisy** brought on a state of **phrensy**. The **brilliancy** of the **daisy**. The **embassy** observed great **secrecy**. He was found guilty of **heresy** and **apostasy**. He **prophesies** indeed, but his **prophecies** are nought. He received a **cornetcy** and then a **lieutenancy**. That **controversy** was not carried on with **courtesy**. She died either of **epilepsy** or **dropsy**.

busy, racy, fancy, leprosy, quinsy, pliancy, phantasy, secrecy, obduracy, proficiency, magistracies, poignancy, ecstasy, idiosyncrasy.

Exercise 106.

Words ending in *re*, chiefly from the French.

In words thoroughly naturalized, the letters have become transposed, as *coffre*, now spelt *coffer*; *cidre*, *cider*.

Filthy **lucre**. The king had his **sceptre**, and the bishop his **mitre**. **Sepulchres** are **sombre** places. The **massacre** of the innocents. **Meagre** fare. What is the **calibre** of those guns? The soldier's **sabre** and other **accoutrements**. The **Caffre** was painted with **ochre**.

ogre, acre, lustre, fibre, metre, spectre, vertibre, (philtre) cylinder, saltpetre, reconnoitre.

N.B.—The *re* final is being gradually transposed into *er*, except in those words in which the spelling would be likely to mislead the pronunciation, as *lucre*, *ogre*, *massacre*, that is, after *c* and *g*.

Exercise 107.

Many words formerly ending in *ck* drop the *k* in their simple form, but resume it with affixes beginning with *e, i, y*. The reason of this is, that *c* has the soft or *s* sound before those vowels, and the *k* is therefore necessary to preserve the original sound.

Monosyllables and their compounds keep the *k*, except in a few foreign words, as *lac of rupees, tic-doloreux*; so also do proper names, as *Frederick*.

traffick, trafficking, trafficker, frolic, frolicking, frolicsome, colic, colicky, picnic, picnicked, bivouac, bivouacking, garlic, garlicky, mimic, mimicking, havoc, critic, laconic, hysteric, hysterically, almanac, cosmetic, physic, physicking, athletic, angelic, despotic, eccentric, fanatic, gigantic, hysterics, narcotic, statistics.

These retain the *k* :—

Warwick, arrack, hillock, &c., cuckoo, cockatoo, cockatrice, crockery, knapsack, cossack, finicking.

Exercise 108.

Words ending in *our* and *or*, as *honour*, *doctor*.

Both come from the Latin, either direct, when the spelling is *or*, or through the French termination in *eur*, when the spelling may be *our*.

The greater part of these words are now spelt with *or*. The spelling of several, whether in *our* or *or*, has been a matter of warm dispute among the learned. The custom of the day, however, seems to favour the spelling in *or*, which, as it exactly represents the sound, and does not conceal the etymology, seems to be more sensible, especially when nearly all of them drop the *u* in composition. The spelling of such words as *honour* (honor), *valour* (valor), is, in fact, a mere matter of taste.

N.B.—American writers, following Webster, always spell these words with *or*.

author, sculptor, tenor, rigour, armour, tumour, vigour, clamour, parlour, ardour, fervour, savour, flavour, vigorous, rigorous, savoury, humorous, clamorous, squalor, honourable, favourite, laborious, invigorate.

Exercise 109.

Words in *ze*, and *se*, *zation*, *sation*.

The former termination is supposed to be derived from the Greek, ending in ιζω; the latter from the French, *iser*.

The spelling of English words with this ending is most irregular. Some words are spelt always with

s, as *advertise* : others always with *z*, as *organize* ; the
greater part, however, are spelt with either *z* or *s*.

Perhaps the best English writers use the *z* the
more frequently, especially when *ize*, like the Latin
termination *fy*, =to make or cause.

advertise, baptize, compromise, idolize, neutralize,
realize, catechize, characterize, paralyze, exercize,
jeopardize, anathematize, enterprize, carbonize, colo-
nize.

Exercise 110.

Terminations in *ance, ence, ant, ent, ancy, ency*,
originally derived from the Latin present participle
in *ans, ens, iens*.

The French present participle ends in *ant*, and
many words which come to us through that language
retain the French spelling : hence the following
anomalies ; *remittent, remittance, independent, dependants, ascendant, ascendency*, &c.

buoyant, brilliant, transient, adherent, accordance,
tendencies, accidence, abhorrence, continent, penance,
assistance, abstinence, resistance, transcendent, diffi-
dence, sufferance, poignancy, consistency, redundancy,
confidants, confidence, dependencies, discrepancy,
preponderance, transparency, belligerent.

Exercise 111.

Terminations in *able, ible, ability, ibility*.

The affix *able* combines with words of either classic
or Saxon origin, as *tractable, laughable*.

The *a* or *i*, however, chiefly depends on the derivation of the word from the Latin adjectives in *abilis,
ibilis*.

peaceable, placable, sensible, suitable, laughable,
risible, legibly, eligible, incredible, traceable, feasible,
indictable, plausible, ostensibly, infallible, transfer-

able, admissible, imperceptibly, advisibility, perfectibility, accessible, impassable,* impassible.*

Exercise 112.

Terminations in *ary*, *ory*. The *a* or *o* depends on the derivation of the word from the Latin forms in *arius*, *orius*, as *necessary*, *transitory*.

oratory, temporary, accessory, accessary,† monitory, monetary, sanitary, sanatory,† customary, hereditary, missionary, desultory, elementary, inventory, incendiary, transitory, lavatory, desultory, plenipotentiary, migratory, &c.

Exercise 113.

Words terminating in *er*, *eer*, *ier*, *yer*, mostly signifying the doer of the action implied in the simple word.

N.B.—Many of these words are spelt *or*, when used as terms in law, as *abettor*, *lessor*.

leveller, abetter, caviller, cavalier, chevalier, muleteer, privateer, auctioneer, pioneer, musketeer, pamphleteer, engineer, fusilier,‡ grenadier, brigadier, buccaneer, gondoleer, bombardeer, cuirassier, mutineer, brazier, glazier, grazier, collier, hosier, cashier, lawyer, sawyer, harrier, pannier, farrier, crozier, glacier, chandelier, gazetteer, registrar (registerer).

---

* Impassable is applied to objects, impassible to character.

† Accessory is the correct spelling, from (Latin) *accessorius*, or (French) *accessoire*. Sanitary is from the Latin *sanitas*, health; sanatory, from *sanator*, sanare (to cure). The root is the same.

‡ This French termination in *ier* is gradually becoming *eer* in English.

SECTION X.

ON THE INFLEXIONS OF WORDS.

(For Rules, see any good Grammar.)[1]

Exercise 114.

Yours truly. **Theirs** for ever. To have **one's** own way. **Sarah's**, the **farmer's daughter's**, shawl. **Harris's**, the **gardener's**, **tulips** and **daisies**. The **tulip's** cup and the **lily's** bell. Two, **dwarfs** were leaning on two **staffs**. With swords and **staves**. The **grottos** were filled with baneful **gases**. **Lilies** of the **valleys**. What **moneys** were due to you? A **moneyed** man. **Honeyed** talk. **Peter's** pence. Three **pennies'** worth of nails. For **prudence'** sake. For **Prudence's** sake. The **Misses** Smith. The **Masters** Brown.* For **righteousness'** sake. For **conscience'** sake. The **Palace** Gardens. The **Princess's** Theatre. The **princesses** sat in the royal box. Her **Majesty's** commands. Their **Majesties'** servants. The Lady **Mayoress's** coach came in collision with the **Duchess's** brougham.

Exercise 115.

A **grouse's** nest. The **porpoise's** pond. An **ostrich's** egg. **Tortoise** shell. A **tortoise's** egg. Her **mistress's** clothes were found in the **gypsy's** tent. A **storied** urn. Three **storeyed** houses. For **goodness'** sake. A poem in twelve **cantos**. Huge

---

* Some say the Miss Smiths and the Master Browns.

folios, quartos, and octavos. The lioness's lair was
empty. Several coveys of partridges were in the
meadow. A pair of ponies. The fairy's gift. Asses'
milk sold here! They mixed the different whiskies
(whiskeys). There have been eight Henrys and two
Marys, sovereigns of England. The donkeys were
grazing in the alleys of the wood. England's allies.
Look at those monkeys. Potatoes and tomatoes. A
cockatrice' egg. Acids effervesce with alkalies.
Tornadoes are frequent in the West Indies. Pease-
pudding. Innuendoes, tyros.*

Exercise 116.

Whose cameos are those? Who's who in 1867?
The ayes and the noes were about equal. If you
don't, it's either because you can't, or you won't.
He wouldn't do it.† The Emperor's aides-de-camp.
An aide-de-camp's duty. Don Quixotte was a satire
on Knights-errant. My three sons-in-law. His
daughter-in-law's book. Three spoonfuls (spoonsful)
every hour. Two or three handfuls. You have left
out an m, or an n. Mind your p's and q's. Are
there two i's or two y's in that word? The Turko-
mans are Mussulmans; many of them wear talis-
mans.

* The rule for the plural of nouns ending in *o*, is to add *es*,
except a vowel precedes the *o*, as *cameos, folios*. *Solos, quartos*,
and a few other words from the Italian, are exceptions.

† In contracted words, such as *can't*, &c., put the apostrophe
in the place of the omitted vowel.

SECTION XI.

List of difficult Words, in their most difficult Forms, for practice by. Dictation.

Asinine	acquiescing	burlesque
annihilated	aiguilettes	benignly
anomalies	antediluvian	browsing
ammonia	Basin ⎫	boulevard
apocalypse	bason ⎭	Bourbonist
aggrandizement	biscuit	Byzantine
amethyst	bullbaiting	Caul
attorneys	barytone	cartel
apocrypha	blamable	catsup (ketchup)
assassination	bagatelle	cereals
amanuensis	battalion	croquet
acolyte	bayoneted	cartouch
aliment	brilliancy	centaur
allopathy	buccaniers	cesspool
armistice	buoyancy	catechism
appraiser	billeted	chamomile
admissible	bulletin	chameleon
alcohol	besieging	chevaux-de-frise
alkalies	burglar	cochineal
alkoran	bankruptcies	condescension
alchymy	beleaguered	conscientious
asparagus	bonneted	cannonier
analytical	Brahma	calomel
apostasy	briar	chouse
auspices	brigadier	commissariat
assignee	bequeathed	commodious

corollary
consummate
cinnamon
chrysalises
canaille
coincidence
cartilage
colliery
connaisseur
cylindrical
cyclopean
cyclopædia
cuirassier
chokeful
cigarette
centering
cenotaph
callous
caliph
colonel
corridor
cameleopard
clayey
cromlech
conciliatory
caterpillar
creases
cynical
chemist }
chymist }
chestnut
Disc, disk
disdained
dahlia
despatch
downfall
dulness

doughty
demise
distich
dawdle
dauphin
drizzling
drollery
domesday
dilemma
dentifrice
diaphragm
damageable
damascene
dishabille
dysentery
dandelion
dromedary
deceitfulness
demeanour
derogatory
dissertation
deaconess
dyspepsia
dishevelled
denizen
demagogue
dynamics
distillation
drivelling
debonair
desultory
diocess—*Times*
diocese—*Alford*
daguerreotype
Eked
epoch
eunuch

ermine
ensuing
elicit
equerry
eligible
enveloped
effervescing
eulogist
eccentric
ecstasy
eclectic
enrolment
enamelled
elision
elysian
embellishment
elliptical
elementary
ebbing
ebony
equipment
eaves-dropper
epidemic
erysipelas ?
encyclopædia
eleemosynary
eel-pie-house
essential, essences
excrescences
excellencies
espousals
escutcheon
exhilarate
etiquette
ecclesiastic
epaulettes
embezzlement

Fraught	gaiety	howitzer
furred	glaciers	hierarchy
feeing	gunwale	hysterical
fee'd	guitar	haberdasher
freed	gamboge	haughtiness
flail	gingham	heinousness
flue	giraffe	hydraulics
feint	gruffness	homeopathic
flagon	garotte	hallelujah
furze	grotesque	hieroglyphics
foretell	galoches	hypocritical
fulness	guillotine	hypercritical
fulsome	gutta percha	hypocondriacal
flannel	gentlemanly	Inquire
frizzle	gazetteer	immure
freighted	geranium	instil
fallible	gymnasium	irony
feasible	gymnastics	icicle
franchise	Hearse	invalid
furlough	haunch	issuing
foreigner	hearth	incense
February	halo	impaired
forfeited	hallo !	indiscreet
fruitfulness	hurdle	instalment
frontispiece	heather	indictment
facetious	heinous	insensible
forestalment	hyssop	idolize
flea-bite	hiccoughs	illiberally
flaccid	hostler	irretrievably
fanaticism	hybrid	imperceptibly
flageolet	handcuff	irreparable
fuchsia	haggard	intelligence
Gloat	hoeing	intolerance
gaudiest	halliards	independence
gorgeous	halcyon	inventory
griffin	hackneyed	incendiary
guano	hyacinth	ichneumon

ipecacuanha
Israelitish
inundation
inanition
Jalap
jeering
jaunting
javelin
jeweller
jasmine }
jessamine }
jaundice
judgment
jungle
juggler
jugular
jonquil
Knoll
knell
knout
knuckle
knickerbockers
knitting
knavishly
knacker
knights-errant
Lye
lewd
luff
lymph
leash
liege
lynx-eyed
lurid
leeward
leopard
laundry

lantern
lodestone
lynch-law
larynx
lessee
lacquered
laurelled
limited
lavander
leisurely
laudanum
liturgy
litany
lyrical
larceny
labyrinth
lolipop
licorice
lozenges
logarithm
lieutenancy
Leicester
Marquee
meerschaum
myrtle
malign
mussel
maudlin
mongrel
maiming
memoirs
moustaches
militia
maccaroni
molasses
mimicked
miniature

menagerie
masquerade
misshapen
massacring
maritime
moneyed
marauders
martyrdom
medallion
mulatto
mythology
mignonette
millennium
machinery
misdemeanour
mortgagee
mausoleum
Mohammedan }
Mahometan }
mosquitos
Mahratta
mediæval
Machiavellian
metempsychosis
Niece
newt
neuter
nuisance
newspapers
neighing
nitre
nauseous
neutralize
novelist
naughtiness
noticeable
naïveté

G

nectarine	prairie	parallelogram
nicety	poignard	periwinkle
Owing	pavilion	pulmonary
oyster	postillion	preliminary
onion	pastille	peremptorily
offspring	phthisis	panegyric
occult	phrensy	peninsula, *sub.*
overseer	pincers	peninsular, *adj.*
orally	parlour	Puseyite
omniscient	pea-hen	Quoit
opossum	prestige	quaint
obsolete	privilege	qualm
obscenity	pinafore	quaff
oscillate	purloined	quash
oxygen	pageantry	quartz
Olympian	partisan	queer
oligarchical	paralyze	quarantine
ostensibly	paralysis	querulous
Odyssey	proselyte	Realm
ophthalmia	palanquin	rhyme
orang-utang	paraffin	route
orangeade	paroxysm	ribbon ⎫
orthoëpy	parallax	riband ⎭
obsequiousness	portmanteau	raisin
obsequies	pariah	recede
orchester	phantasies	raiment
opaque	paradise	routine
oblique	porcelain	rupee
omen	picaback	ruffian
ominous	premises	ribald
Pyre	philanthropist	recipe
parsley	pentateuch	recurring
palings	phosphorescent	rescuing
pacha ⎫	perfectibility	ricochet
pasha ⎭	pusillanimous	rehearsal
peevish	presbyterian	repartee
phœnix	plenipotentiary	roguery

requisite
raspberry
reprieved
reimbursed'
reconnoitring
reservoir
receivable
Salve
sooty
sphinx
slough
skewer
sluices
screech-owl
skirmish
surtout
sortie
surname
saucer
smallness
stillness
sombre
stiffness
squeamish
surfeit
syringe
syrupy
scoundrel
sapphire
shepherd
suttler
styptic
sword-knot
saccharine
skeleton
subaltern
sulphurous

sacrament
sacrilege
sepulchre
strategy
stupefy
sacrifice
scepticism
suggestion
shivering
solicited
synagogue
solemnized
synonyme
spasmodic
scrupulous
schismatic
superseded
summarily
sycamore
surveillance
synonymous
spermaceti
subterranean
scarlatina
Tyre
Tsar }
Czar }
'tisn't
taboo
tattooed
thraldom
terrace
tassel
tortoise
tariff
tingeing
tonsil

tenant
turquoise
trysting-place
tactitian
teetotaller
teetotalism
transcendent
transferable
Tsarévitch
troubadour
theatric
tragedian
tantamount
tobacco
Umble-pie
unique
unwieldy
unravelled
uncancelled
unconscionable
unembarrassed
untramelled
unequivocably
unparalleled
usquebaugh
Unitarian
Vie
vying
vaunt
valid
vague
vogue
vengeance
vaccine
venison
viscid
vitriol

villain
venomous
vehicle
visitors
vaudeville
villany
villenage
vinaigrette
vermicelli
variegated
velocipede
verdigris
vaccination
violoncello
veterinary
Wan
whoa ?

waive
wiry
wreak
weapon
wilful
whilom
woful
waggon (wagon)
whisky
whiskies
wainscot
wayfarer
warren
witticism
whitewashing
Yew
yacht

yule
yearn
yeast
yawl
yeoman
yclept
yawning
Zinc
zigzag
zealous
zebra
zouave
zephyr
zenith
zoophite
zoological

PROPER NAMES.

Abel
Æneas
Apollo
Aaron
Achilles
Apocalypse
Apocrypha
Aleppo
Azores
Anglesey
Amoor (Amur)
Apennines
Aylesbury
Abyssinia
Aix-la-Chapelle
Aberystwith

Baal
Balaam
Bacchus
Brahmin
Babylon
Britannia
Britain
Brittany
Baalbec
Bayonne
Blenheim
Boulogne
Bokhara
Bordeaux
Brussels
Badajoz

Babelmandeb
Buenos Ayres
Cæsar
Canaan
Cyprus
Cabool (Cabul)
Cairo
Ceylon
Chili
Coblenz
Cologne
Castille
Cayenne
Cashmere
Carlisle
Canaries

Cevennes
Caernarvon
Caermarthen
Czech (tchek)
Cartagena
Champagne
Chesapeake
Cincinnati
Cirencester
Columbia
Corunna
Dulwich
Drogheda (Dro-
heda)
Elisha
Evesham
Frederick
Fahrenheit
Figi (Feejee)
Greece
Ghauts
Giaour
Geneva
Guelph
Ghibeline
Gibraltar
Gloucester
Guiana
Hegira
Harwich
Havanna
Hanover
Hertford
Hamburg
Homburg

Halifax
Hanseatic
Himalaya
Habakkuk
Jalapa }
Xalapa }
Jeres }
Xeres }
Jehovah
Jezabel
Judæa
Kamtschatka
Ládoga
Lloyd
Llewellyn
Llandudno
Lebanon
Leicester
Lerwick
Michael
Messiah
Maccabæus
Maccabees
Maelstrom
Magellan
Madeira
Manilla
Marseilles
Marlborough
Mahratta
Mediterranean
Massachusetts
Mississippi
Mosquito
Merthyr Tydvil

Nineveh
Nebuchadnezzar
Pharaoh
Philistine
Phrygian
Pennsylvania
Philadelphia
Philippines
Peloponnesus
Pyrenees
Pyrrhus
Piræus
Phœnicia
Phœbus
Philip*
Raphael
Russell
Rheims
Ryswick
Rouen
Ramillies
Rio Janeiro
Styx
Sphynx
Scythian
Seine
Sahara
Seville
Sutlej
Seidlitz
Singapore
Sadducees
Tyne
Tonquin
Tahiti

* Why is Port Phillip so spelt? See Newspapers and Shipping Advertisements.

Teneriffe	Valparaiso	Yeso (Jesso)
Tuilleries	Van Diemen's	Zutphen
Tyrolese	Weymouth	Zuyder Zee
Utrecht	Xantippe	
Valenciennes	Yedo (Jeddo)	

APPENDIX

FEW CHANGES have taken place in the orthography of the English language since the time of Johnson, and those but trifling ones. Perhaps, in the present day, there are about from 1,800 to 2,000 words, the spelling of which, either in their simple or inflected forms, is unsettled. In the foregoing Exercises, nearly all these will be found spelt in the manner which seems most usual in current literature.

Before the time of Johnson, back to that of Elizabeth, the public had excellent models on which to frame their spelling, in Addison, Pope, Dryden, Milton, Shakespere, and in the translation of the Bible. Yet the spelling of the mass of educated people was so faulty in the seventeenth and greater part of the eighteenth century, that the private letters of the ladies and gentlemen of that period would now serve as exercises for schoolboy correction.

From the age of Elizabeth to that of Edward III. was the period of so-called middle, or mixed, or compound English. During this time, the amalgamation of the different elements of our language was perfected. Some authors seem to have tried experiments in spelling; others wrote down their words as they were pronounced. The invention of printing at first added to the confusion of English spelling. Foreigners were employed to cut the type, and in their ignorance of the language, perverted the spelling, substituting often one letter for another, especially y and g. This confusion was increased when the black letter was changed for the modern type, so that, in the earlier printed books, it is no uncommon thing to find the same word spelt in a dozen different ways. It was only in the reign of Elizabeth and James I. that something like uniformity in spelling came forth from that chaos of letters with which words had been hitherto built up.

From 1350 to 1250 was the period of Old English; and from 1250 to 1150 that of semi-Saxon.

From 1150 to about 600 was the time of the Anglo-Saxon, the chief literary productions of which are the writings of Alfric, Archbishop of Canterbury, *circa* 1006, and of Alfred the Great, together with the Saxon chronicles and laws. To understand these requires a glossary, and some special study of the Anglo-Saxon grammar.

It is intended that the following extracts should be re-written by the pupil in modern orthography, without changing either the structure of the sentences, or any of the words, except those that are altogether out of use. The meaning of these, where it is considered necessary, will be found in the notes.

BEN JONSON. 1574—1637.

You'll bring your head within a cockscomb will you ?
Or a knight of the curious coxcomb.
Whom not a Puritan in Blackfriers will touch so much as for a feather.
What do you think of me ? that I'm a chiause.
You must think he may have a receit to make hair come.
Yes! here are six score Edwards shillings, and an old Harry's sovereign.—Very good.—And three James shillings and an Elizabeth groat, just twenty nobles.—O! you are too just, I would you had the other noble in Maries.—I have some Philip and Maries.

Clean linnen.—Sallads and mushromes.

I ha' staid too long.—More prophane and cholerick than your glassmen.

Brimstone and arsnick.—And I'm a batchelor, worth nought.—Truely I do not like the dullness of your eye.—Golden flaggons.—He borrowed a sute.—By vertue of my office.—What shall I do? I'm catched.—You raskal.

SPENSER. 1553—1599.

VIEW OF THE STATE OF IRELAND. 1596.

Truely this is a great inconvenience and a great cause of the maintenance of theeves, knowing their receivers alwayes ready; for, were there no receivers, there would be no theeves; but this (me seemes) might easily be provided for, that the receiver being convicted by good proofes might receive his tryall without the principall.

I cannot deny but that aunciently it (the mantle) was common to most (peoples), and yet sithence disused and laide away. But in this later age of the world, it was renewed and brought in again by those northerne nations, when breaking out of their cold caves, and frozen habitations into the sweet soyle of Europe, they brought with them their usual weedes, fit to shield the cold and that continual frost, to which they had at home been inured.

FAIRIE QUEEN.

BOOK I. CANTO I.

A GENTLE knight was pricking on the plaine,
Ycladd in mightie armes and silver shielde,
Wherein old dints of deepe woundes did remaine,
The cruel markes of many' a bloody fielde;
Yet armes till that time did he never wield;
His angry steede did chide his foming bitt,
As much disdayning to the curbe to yield:
Full iolly knight he seemd, and faire did sitt,
As one for knightly giusts and fierce encounters fitt.

And on his brest a bloodie crosse he bore,
The deare remembrance of his dying Lord,
For whose sweete sake that glorious badge he wore,
And dead, as living, ever him ador'd:
Upon his shield the like was also scor'd,
For soveraine hope, which in his helpe he had.
Right, faithfull, true he was in deede and word;
But of his cheere did seeme too solemne sad;
Yet nothing did he dread, but ever was ydrad.

A lovely ladie rode him faire beside
Upon a lowly asse more white then snow;
Yet she much whiter; but the same did hide
Under a vele, that wimpled was full low;
And over all a blacke stole shee did throw,
As one that inly mournd; so was she sad,
And heavie sate upon her palfrey slow;
Seemed in heart some hidden care she had;
And by her in a line a milke-white lambe she lad.

So pure and innocent, as that same lambe,
She was in life and every vertuous lore,
And by descent from royall lynage came
Of ancient kinges and queenes, that had of yore
Their scepters stretcht from east to westerne shore,
And all the world in their subjection held;
Till that infernal feend with foule uprore
Forwasted all their land, and them expeld;
Whom to avenge, she had this knight from far compeld.

Behind her farre away a dwarfe did lag,
That lasie seemd, in being ever last,
Or wearied with bearing of her bag
Of needments at his backe. Thus as they past,
The day with cloudes was suddeine overcast,
And angry Iove an hideous storme of raine
Did poure into his lemans lap so fast,
That everie wight to shrowd it did constrain;
And this faire couple eke to shroud themselves were fain.

Enforst to seeke some covert nigh at hand,
A shadie grove not farr away they spide,

`That promist ayde the tempest to withstand;
Whose loftie trees, yclad with sommers pride
Did spred so broad, that heavens light did hide,
Not perceable with power of any starr;
And all within were pathes and alleies wide,
With footing worne, and leading inward farr:
Faire harbour that them seems; so in they entred ar.

And foorth they passe, with pleasure forward led,
Ioying to heare the birdes sweete harmony,
Which therein shrouded from the tempest dred,
Seemd in their song to scorne the cruell sky.
Much can they praise the trees so straight and hy
The sayling pine, the cedar proud and tall;
The vine-propp elme, the poplar never dry;
The builder oake, sole king of forrests all;
The aspine good for staves, the cypresse funerall;

The laurell, meed of mightie conquerours
And poets sage; the firre that weepeth still;
The willow, worne of forlorne paramours;
The eugh, obedient to the benders will;
The birche for shaftes, the sallow for the mill;
The mirrhe sweete-bleeding in the bitter wound;
The warlike beech, the ash for nothing ill:
The fruitful olive, and the platane round;
The carver holme, the maple, seldom inward sound.

Led with delight, they thus beguile the way,
Untill the blustring storme is overblowne;
When, weening to returne, whence they did stray,
They cannot finde that path, which first was showne,
But wander too and fro in waies unknowne,
Furthest from end then, when they neerest weone,
That makes them doubt their wits be not their owne.
So many paths, so many turnings seene,
That which of them to take in diverse doubt they been.

SIR THOMAS MORE. 1480—1535.

Descripcion of Richarde the Thirde.

Richarde, the thirde sonne of Richarde, Duke of York, was in witte and courage egall with his two brothers, in bodye and prowesse farre vnder them bothe, little of stature, ill fetured of limmes, croke backed, his left shoulder much higher than his right, hard fauoured of visage, and such as is in states called warlye, in other menne otherwise, he was malicious, wrathfull, enuious, and from afore his birth, euer frowarde.

．　　　．　　　．　　　．　　　．　　　．　　　．

When these lordes with diuerse other of bothe the parties were comme in presence, the kynge liftinge vppe himselfe and vndersette with pillowes, as it is reported on this wyse sayd vnto them, ' My lordes, my dere kinsmenne and alies, in what plighte I lye you see, and I feele. By whiche the lesse whyle I looke to lyue with you, the more depelye am I moued to care in what case I leaue you, for such as I leaue you, suche bee my children lyke to fynde you. Whiche if they shoulde (that Godde forbydde) fynde you at varyaunce, myght happe to fall themselfe at warre ere their discrecion woulde serue to sette you at peace. Ye se their youthe, of whiche I recken the onely suretie to reste in youre concord. For it suffiseth not that al you loue them, yf eche of you hate other. If they wer menne, your faithfulnesse happelye woulde suffise. But childehood must be maintained by mens authoritye, and slipper youth vnder-propped with elder counsayle, which neither they can haue, but ye geue it, nor ye geue it, if ye gree not. For what eche laboureth to breake that the other maketh, and for hatred of ech of others parson, impugneth eche others counsayle, there must it nedes bee long ere anye good conclusion goe forwarde. And also while either partye laboureth to be chiefe, flattery shall haue more place then plaine and faithfull aduyse, of whiche muste needes ensue the euyll bringing vppe of the prynce, whose mynd in tender youth infect, shal redily fal to mischief and riot, and drawe down with this noble realme to ruine, but if grace turn him to wisdom: which if God send, then thei that by euill menes before pleased hym best, shal after fall farthest out of fauour, so that euer at length euill driftes dreue to nought, and good plain wayes prosper.

TYNDAL. 1526.

Lord's Prayer.

Oure Father which arte in heven, halowed be thy name. Let thy kingdom come. Thy will be fulfilled, as well in erth, as hit is in heven. Geve us this daye oure dayly breade. And forgeve vs oure treaspases even as we forgeve them which treaspas vs. Leede vs not into temptacion, but delyvre vs from yvell. Amen.

STEPHEN HAWES. *Circa* 1495.

Pastime of Plesure.

I sawe come ridyng in a valley farre
A goodly ladye, environned about
With tongues of fire, as bright as any starre
That fiery flambes, ensensed al way out
Whiche I behelde, and was in great doubt,
Her palfrey swift, rennyng as the winde
With two white greyhoūds, that were not behind.

When that these greyhoundes had me so espied
With faunyng chere of great humilitie
In goodly haste, they fast unto me hied;
I mused why, and wherfore it shoulde be,
But I welcomed them, in every degree;
They leaped oft, and were of me right faine,
I suffred them, and cherished them againe.

Their collers were of golde and of tyssue fine
Wherin their names appeared by scripture
Of dyamondes that clerely do shine;
The letters were grauen fayre and pure;
To reade their names, I did my busye cure:
The one was Gouernaunce, the other named Grace,
Then was I gladde of all this sodayne cace.

And then the ladye, with fiery flambe
Of brennyng tongues, was in my presence
Upon her palfrey, whiche had unto name
Pegase the swifte, so faire in excellence
Whiche sometime longed with his preminence
To kyng Percius, the sonne of Jupiter
On whom he rode by the worlde so farre.

To me she saied, she marueyled muche why
That her greyhoundes shewed me that fauoure;
What was my name, she asked me truely.
To whom I saied : it was La Graunde Amoure
Besechyng you to be to me succoure
To the tower of Doctrine, and also me tell
Your proper name, and where you do dwell.

My name, quod she, in all the world is knowen;
I clipped[1] Fame in every region,
For I my horne in sundrye wise haue blowen
After the deathe of many a champion
And with my tongues have made aye mencion
Of their great actes, agayne to revive
In flamyng tongues, for to abide on live.

GEOFFREY CHAUCER.

FROM THE BOOK OF THE TALIS OF CANTERBURY.

(Printed by Caxton. Black Letter in Grenville Library, 1st Edit.,
1475–76, so considered by Tyrrwhit and Ames.)

And fil[2] in that seson[3] on a day,
In Suthwerk atte tabard as I lay,
Redy to wende on my pilgremage
To Cauntirbury, with denout corage,
That night was come into that hosterye,
Wel nyne and twenty in a companye;
Of sondry folk be auenture y falle,
In feleship as pilgrymys were they alle

---

[1] Yclept. Old English, past part.   [2] it befell.   [3] Apprill.

That toward Cauntirbury wolden ryde.
The chambris and the stablis were wyde:
And wel were they esid atte beste,
And shortly whan the sonne was at reste,
So had I spokyn with hem euerichon,
That I was of her feleship anon;
And made forward erly for to ryse,
To take our wey there as I you deuyse.
But natheles whiles that y haue tyme and space,
Or that y ferthir in this tale pace;
Me thinketh that it were accordaunt to reson,
To telle you al the condicion,
Of eche of hem so as it semed me,
And whiche they were and of what degree;
And in what aray eke they weren ynne,
And at a knyght I will begynne.

CAXTON.

(From First Edition, in British Museum.)

THE GAME AND PLAYE OF THE CHESSE.

This first chapiter of the first tractate showeth under what kynge the play of the chesse was founden and maad.

Amonge all the euyll condicions and signes that may be in a man the first and y grettest is what he feereth not, ne dredeth to displese and make wroth God by synne, and the peple lyuying disordynatly, what he reccheth not, ner taketh hede vnto them that repreue hym and his vices, but sleeth them. In suche wyse as did the emperour Nero whiche dide do[1] slee his maister seneyue, for as moche as he might not suffre to be repreuid and taught of hym. In lyke wyse was somtyme a kynge in Babiloine that was named Emsmerodach, a jolye man with oute justice, and so cruell that he dyde do hewe his fathers body in thre honderd pieces, and gaf hit to ete and deuour to thre honderd Brides that men calle voultres, and was of suche condicion as was Nero, and right well resemblid and was lyke

[1] to.

vnto his fader Nabogodonosor, whiche on a tyme wold do
slee alle the sage and wyse men of Babylonye, for as
moche as they coude not telle hym his dreme that he had
dremed on a nyght and had forgoten hit, lyke as it is wreton
in the bible in the book of danyell. Under this kynge
than Emsmerodach was this game and playe of the chesse
founden. Trewe it is that some men wene[1] that this playe
was founden in the tyme of the bataylles and siege of
Troye. But that is not soo. For this playe cam to the
playes of the caldees as dyomedes the Greek sayth and
reherceth. That amonge the philosophrs was the most
renomed playe amonge all other playes. And after that
cam this playe in the time of Alexandre the Grete in to
Egipte, and so vnto alle the parties toward the south.
And the cause wherfore thys playe was so renomed shall
be sayd in the thirde Chapitre.

GEOFFREY CHAUCER. 1375.

PATIENT GRISILDE.

Among this pore folk there duelt a man,
Which that was holden porest of hem alle;
But heighe God som tyme sende can
His grace unto a litel oxe stalle.
Janicula men of that throp him calle.
A doughter had he, fair y-nough to sight,
And Grisildes this yonge mayden hight.

But for to speke of hir vertuous beaute,
Than was sche oon the fayrest under sonne;
For porely i-fostered up was sche,
No licorous lust was in hir body ronne;
Wel ofter of the welle than of the tonne
Sche dronk, and for sche wolde vertu please,
Sche knew wel labour, but noon ydel ease.

But though this mayden tender were of age,
Yet in the brest of her virginite
Ther was enclosed rype and sad corrage;
And in gret reverence and charite

---

[1] think (ween).

Hir olde pore fader fostered sche ;
A fewe scheep spynnyng on the feld sche kept,
Sche nolde not ben ydel til sche slept.
  And whan she com hom sche wolde brynge
Wortis and other herbis tymes ofte,
The which sche schred and seth for her lyvyng,[1]
And made hir bed ful hard, and no thing softe.
And aye sche kept hir fadres lif on lofte,[2]
With every obeissance and diligence, •
That child may do to fadres reverence.
  Upon Grisildes, the pore creature,
Ful ofte sithes this marquys set his ye,
As he on huntyng rood peraventure.
And whan it fel he mighte hir espye,
He not with wantoun lokyng of foyle
His eyghen cast upon hir, but in sad wyse
Upon hir cheer he wold him oft avise,
  Comendyng in his hert hir wommanhede,
And eek hir vertu, passyng other wight
Of so yong age, as wel in cheer as dede.
For though the poeple have no gret insight
In vertu, he considereth aright
Hir bounté, and desposed that he wolde
Wedde hir oonly, if ever he wedde scholde.

JOHN DE TREVISA. 1387.

Southern Dialect.

DESCRIPTION OF BRITAIN.

  As Fraunce passeth Britayn, so Brytain passeth Irlond yn
fayr weder and nobleté, bute noght yn helthe; for this
ylond ys best to brynge forthe tron, and fruyt, and rotheron,[3]
and othere bestes, and wyn groweth ther-ynne in som
places. The lond hath plenté of foules and of bestes, of
dyvers manere kinde ; the lond ys plentuos and the se also ;

---

[1] Which she sliced and *boiled*, or *seethed* for her food.
[2] On high, *i.e.* she supported him.
[3] oxen.

H

the lond ys noble, copious, and ryche of noble welles, and
of noble ryvers with plenté of fysch. Thar ys gret plenté
of smal fysch and of eeles, so that cherles in som place
feedeth sowes with fysch. Thar buth ofte ytake dolphyns,
and se-calves, and balenes, (gret fysch, as hyt were of
whaales kunde) and dyvers manere schyl-fysch, among the
whoche schyl-fysch buth moskles that habbeth withynne
ham (margey) perles of al manere colour of[1] hugh,[2] of
rody and red, of purpre and of blugh,[3] and specialych and
moost of whyte. Thar ys also plenté of schyl-fysch that
me dyeth with fyn reed; the rednes ther-of ys wondre fayr
and stable, and steyneth nevere with cold ne with heete,
with weete ne with drythe, bote evere the elther the hu ys
the veyrer; that buth also salt welles and hoote welles,
ther-of eorneth stremes of hoot bathes, to-deled[4] in dyvers
places accordyng for man and womman, and for al maner
age, yong and olde.

Thar buth scheep that bereth good wolle; thar buth
meny hertes and wylde bestes, and fewe wolves, therfore
scheep buth the more sykerlyche,[5] safe withoute kepynge
ylefte yn the foold; and yn this ylond also but hmeny cites
and tounes faire, noble, and ryche; meny grete ryvers and
stremes with gret plenté of fysch; meny fayre wodes and
grete with wel meny bestes, tame and wylde. The eorthe
of that lond ys copious of metayl oor and of salte welles;
of quareres of marbel, of dyvers manere stones, of reed, of
whyt, of nasche,[6] of hard, of chalk, and of whyt lym;
thar ys also whyt cley and reed for to make of crokkes and
steenes and other vessel, and barnd tyyl to hele[7] with hous
and churches, as hyt were in the other Samia that hatte
Samos. Also Flaundres loveth the wolle of this lond, and
Normandy the skynnes and the fellys; Gaskuyn the yre[8]
and the leed; Irlond the oor and the salt; al Europa loveth
and desireth the whyte metayl of this lond.

Brytayn hath ynow of al matyr that neodeth bugge[9] and
sulle, other is neodfol to mannes use; thar lakketh nevere

---

[1] Harl. MS. reads *and hewe*. [2] For *hw* or *hew.*
[3] For *blw* or *blewe.*   [4] divided.   [5] safe.   [6] soft.
[7] cover.   [8] iron.   [9] buy.

salt and yre, tharfore a versefyour in hys metre preyseth this lond in this manere :—

Engelond ys good lond fruytfol of the wolle, bote[1] a kornere ! Engleond fol of pley ! freomen wel worthy to pleye ! freomen, freo tonges, the hert*e* freo ! Freo buth[2] alle the leden ;[3] here hond ys more freo, more betre than here tonge.

JOHN WYCLIF or WYCLIFFE. 1375.

FROM YE EUUANGELIE OF JOON.

Aftir thes thinges Jhesu wente ouer the see of galilee, that is tiberiadis, and a greet multitude suede hym, for thei sighen the tokenes that he dide on them that weren sijk. Therfore Jhesu wente into an hil, and satte there with his disciplis. For so the Pask was ful nygh, a feest day of the iewis. Therfore whanne Jhesu hadde lifte vp the yghen[4] and had seen for a greet multitude came to him, he seith to philip, wherof schulen we bie loues, that thes men ete. Sothely he seyde this thing temptynge hym, forsothe he wiste what was to do. Philip answeride to hym, the looues of two hundride pens sufficen not to them that eche man take a litil what. One of his disciplis andrewe the brother of symount ·petre seith to hym, one childe is here that hath fyue barly looues and two fischis, but what ben thes thingis amonge so many men. Therfore Jhesu seith, make yee men for to sitte at the mete ; for there was myche hay in the place. Therfore men saten at the mete in nowmbre of fyue thousandis. Therfore Jhesu took the fyue looues, and whanne he had done thankyngis, he departide to men sittynge at the mete, also and of the fischis, as myche as thei wolden;·forsothe as thei ben fulfilde. he seyde to his disciplis, gader yee the relifes that ben lefte, that thei perische not. Therfore thei gaderiden and fillide twelue cofyns[5] of relifes of the fyue barly loues and two fisches that leften to them that hadden eten. Therfore the men whanne they hadden seen the token (or myracle) that he had done, seyden, for this is verreyley a prophete that is com into the worlde.

[1] to boot.   [2] are.   [3] tongues.   [4] eyes.
[5] coffins, boxes.

FROM THE 'BRUCE' OF BARBOUR.

(Lowland Scotch. Written about 1365.)

A ! fredome is a noble thing,—
Fredome mayss man to haiff liking;
Fredome all solace to man giffis:
He levys at ess that frely levys!
A noble hart may haiff nane ess,
Na[1] ellys nocht[1] that may him pless,
Gyff fredome failyhe : for fre liking
Is yharnyt[2] our all othir thing.
Na he, that ay hass levyt fre,
May nocht knaw weill the propyrté,
The angyr, na the wrechyt dome,
That is cowplyt to foule thyrldome.
But gyff he had assayit it,
Than all perquer[3] he suld it wyt;[4]
And suld think fredome mar to pryss,
Than all the gold in warld that is.
Thus contrar thingis euir mar
Discoweryngis off the tothir ar.
And he that thryll is has nocht his ;
All that he hass embandownyt is
Till[5] hys Lord, quhat[6] euir he be.
Yheyt has he nocht sa mekill[7] fre
As fre wyll to leyve, or do
That at his hart hym drawis to.

And thryldome is weill wer than deid ;[8]
For quhill a thryll his lyff may leid,
It merrys[9] him, body and banys ;
And dede anoyis him bot anys.[10]
Schortly to say, is nane can tell
The halle conditioun off a threll.

---

[1] Na, nocht, double negative.   [2] desired.   [3] exactly.
[4] shun.   [5] to.   [6] quhat; *qu* in N. dialects = *w*.
[7] much.   [8] death.   [9] mars.   [10] once.

FROM THE VISION OF PIERS PLOWMAN.

(Mixed Southern and Midland Dialect. Written about 1362.

In a somer seson
Whan softe was the Sonne
I shoop[1] me into shroudes[2]
As I a sheep[3] weere,
In habite as an heremite
Unholy of Werkes,
Wente wide in this world
Wondres to here;
Ac on a May morwenynge
On Malverne hilles
Me bifel a ferly[4]
Of fairye me thoghte.
I was very for-wandred,[5]
And wente me to reste
Under a brood bank
By a bournes syde;
And as I lay and lenede
And loked on the watres,
I slombred into a slepyng,
It sweyed[6] so murye.[7]
Thanne gan I meten
A merveillous swevene,[8]
That I was in a wildernesse
Wist I nevere where;
And as I beheeld into the Eest
An heigh to the sonne,
I seigh a tour on a toft[9]
Trieliche[10] y-maked,
A deep dale bynethe,
A dongeon therinne
With depe diches and derke
And dredfulle of sighte.

[1] shaped. [2] clothes. [3] shepherd. [4] wonder.
[5] worn out with wandering; *for* = Germ. *ver*.
[6] sounded. [7] pleasantly. [8] dream.
[9] An open exposed place. [10] choicely.

A fair feeld ful of folk
Fond I ther bitwene,
Of alle manere of men,—
The meene and the riche,
Werchynge and wandrynge
As the world asketh.

. . . . .

SIR JOHN MANDEVILLE.   *Circa* 1356.

(From first printed Edition, in black letter, in Grenville Library,
Brit. Mus.   Midland Dialect.)

INTRODUCTION TO TRAVELS.

He that woll passe ouer the se, he may go many weyes
bothe on londe and see after the countrees that he comethe
fro : and many of theym come all to one ende.   But
trowest nat that I woll tell all the townes and cytes and
castellys that men shall go by, for than shulde I make to
longe tale, but all only some countres and moost pryncypall
steddes[1] that men shall goo thoroughe to go the right wey.

. . . .

THE BEDOUINS.

These men that I speke of they tyll nat the londe for
they ete no brede, but if[2] it be any that dwell nere a
goode towne ;—and they rost all their fysshes and flesshe
upon hote stones ageyne the son—and they ar stronge
men and well fightynge, and they do no thynge but
chase wylde bestis for their sustenaunce—and they sette
nat by theyr lyues, and therfore they drede not the Soudan
nor none other prynce of all the worlde.   And they haue
oft werre wyth the Soudan, and that same time that I was
dwellynge wyth hym, they bare nat but a sheelde and
spere for to defende theym wyth.   And they holde none
other armours, but they wynde their hedes and their neckes
in a great lynen clothe, and they are men full yll kynde.

[1] Gr. *stadt*, places.   .   [2] except that.

RICHARD ROLLE DE HAMPOLE.

(About A.D. 1340.   North Country Dialect.)

THE PRICKE OF CONSCIENCE.

DEATH.

Four skilles[1] I fynd writen in som stede,[2]
Why men suld specialy drede the dede;
An[3] es for the dede stoure[4] swa felle[5]
That es mare payne than man can telle,
The whilk ilk[6] man sal fele within,
When the body and the saule salle twyn.[7]
Another es for the sight that he sal se
Of devels, that about hym than salle be.
The thred[8] es for the acount that he sal yheld
Of alle his lyf, of yhouthe and elde.
The ferth[9] es, for he is uncertayne
Whether he sal wend til ioy or payne.

   .   .   .   .   .

First aght men drede the ded in hert,
For the payn of the dede that es swa smert,
That es the hard stour at the last ende,
When the saule sal fra the body wende;
A doleful partyng es that to telle,
For thai luf ay togyder to duelle;
Nouther of tham wald other forga,
Swa mykel[10] lof es bytwen than twa;
And the mare that twa togyder lufes,
Als a man and his wyfe oft pruves,
The mare sorow and murnying
By-hoves be at thair departyng.
Bot the body and the saul with the lyfe
Lufes mare samen[11] than man and his wyfe,
Whether thai be in gude way or ille,
And that es for many sere[12] skylle.

---

[1] reasons. [2] places. [3] one. [4] agony.
[5] dreadful. [6] each. [7] twain (part).
[8] third. [9] fourth. [10] much.
[11] together (Germ. zusammen). [12] diverse.

ROBERT OF GLOUCESTER. *Circa* A.D. 1300.

(From the Legend of Gilbert à Becket, father of Thomas à
Becket. Southern Dialect.)

And nameliche[1] thurf[2] a maid
That this Gilbert lovede faste,
The Prince's douchter admiraud
That hire hurte al upe[3] him caste.

. . . . .

And eschtë[4] him of Engelonde,
And of the manere there,
And of the lyf of Cristene men,
And what here bileve were.
The manere of Engelonde
This Gilbert hire tolde fore,
And the toun het[5] Londone
That he was inne[6] ibore,[7]
And the bileve of Cristene men
This blisse withouten ende,
In hevene shall here medï[8] beo,
Whan hi[9] schulle henne[10] wende.
'Ich wole' heo[11] seide 'al mi lond
Leve for love of the,
And Cristene womman become,
If thu wolt spousi me.'

BRUT OF LAYAMON.

(From a Manuscript of the thirteenth Century. Southern
Dialect.)

RETURN OF ARTHUR.

Wind heom[12] stod on willen;
weder alfe heo[13] wolden.
blithe hee weoren alle for thi;[14]
up heo comen at Grimesbi.

[1] especially (Germ. namentlich).　　[2] through.
[3] upon.　　[4] asked.　　[5] hight.　　[6] in it.
[7] born.　　[8] meed.　　[9] they.　　[10] hence.
[11] she.　　[12] them.　　[13] whether as they.
[14] therefore.

thæt iherden[1] sone[2]
tha haehste[3] of thissen londe.
and to thære quene com tidende
of Arthure than kinge ;
that he wes isund icumen
and his folc ō selen.[4]
Tha weoren inne Bruttene
blissin inoge ;[5]
her wes fitheling and song,
her wes harpinge among,
pipen and bemen,[6]
murie ther sungen.
Scopes[7] ther sungen
of Arthure than kingen,
and of than muchele wurth-scipe
the[8] he iwunnen[9] hafeden.[10]
folc cō to hirede[11]
of seole cunne theode ;[12]
Widen and siden
folc wes on selen.[13]
all that Arthur isæh,[14]
al hit him to baeh ;[15]
riche men and pouere,
swa the hagel[16] ualleth.[17]
nes ther nan swa wrecche Brut,[18]
that he nes awælged.[19]
Her mon mai arede[20]
of Arthure than king,
hu he twelf yere
seothen[21] wuneden[22] here,
Inne grithe[23] and inni Fride,[24]
in alle uægernesse.[25]

---

[1] that heard. [2] soon. [3] the highest. [4] prosperity.
[5] enough (Germ. genug). [6] trumps.
[7] makers or poets. [8] that.
[9] won (Germ. gewonnen). [10] had. [11] in concourse.
[12] from several kinds of lands. [13] prosperity.
[14] saw. [15] obey. [16] hail. [17] falleth.
[18] Briton. [19] enriched. [20] tell. [21] afterwards.
[22] dwelt, (Germ. wohnen). [23] peace. [24] amity.
[25] fairness.

Na man him ne faht[1] with,
no he ne makede nan unfrid,[2]
ne mihte nauere[3] nan man
bi-thenchen[4] of blissen,
that weoren in ai theode[5]
mare han i thisse.
ne miht nauere[6] mon cūne[7]
nan swa muchel wunne,[8]
swa wes mid Arthure,
and mid his folke here.

A PROCLAMATION OF HENRY III. A.D. 1258.

Henry, thurg Godes fultome,[9] king on Engleneloande,
Lhoaurd on Yrloand, Duke on Normand, on Acquitain,
Eorl on Anjou, send I greting to alle hise holde,[10] ilaerde[11]
and ilewerde[12] on Huntingdonschiere. That witen ge well
alle, thaet we willen and unnen[13] thaet ure raedesmen[14] alle
other, the moare del of heom, that beoth[15] ichosen thurg us
and thurg thaet laendesfolk on our Kuneriche,[16] habbith
idon,[17] und schullen[18] don, in the worthnes of God and ure
threowthe,[19] for the freme[20] of the loande, thurg the besigte[21]
of than toforen[22] iseide raedesmen, beo stedefæst and iles-
tinde[23] in all thinge a butan[24] ænde.

DEDICATION OF THE ORMULUM. A.D. 1229.

(Called so after Orm, or Ormin, the writer. Northern Dialect.*)

Nu, brotherr Wallterr, brotherr min
Affter the flæshess kinde;
And brotherr min in Chrisstenndom

[1] fought.	[2] strife.	[3] never.	[4] bethink.
[5] any land.	[6] never.	[7] know (ken).	[8] joy.
[9] support.	[10] subjects.	[11] learned.	[12] unlearned.
[13] grant.	[14] counsellors.	[15] be.	[16] kingdom.
[17] done.	[18] shall.	[19] troth (allegiance).	[20] good.
[21] determination.	[22] afore.	[23] permanent.	[24] without.

* The spelling of this work should be noted. The double
consonants are intended to show that the preceding vowel is
short; whereas, before a single consonant the vowel was pro-

Thurrh falluhht[1] and thurrh trowwthe ;
& brotherr min in Godess hus,
Yet o[2] the thride wise,[3]
Thurrh thatt witt[4] hafenn takenn ba[5]
An reghellboc[6] to folghenn,[7]
Unnderr Kanunnkess[8] had[9] and lif,
Swa summ[10] Sannt Awwstin sette ;
Ice hafe don swa summ thu badd
& forthedd[11] te thin wille,
Icc hafe wennd[12] inntill Ennglissh
Goddspelless hallghe[13] láre,
Affterr thatt little witt tatt me
Min Drihhtin[14] hafethth lenedd.[15]
Thu thohhtesst tatt it mihhte wel
Till mikell frame[16] turrnenn,
Yiff Ennglissh follk, forr lufe off Crist,
Itt wollde gerne lernenn,
& follghenn itt, & fittenn itt
Withth thohtht, withth word, withth dede.

EXTRACTS FROM SAXON CHRONICLE. *Circa* 1154.

Hi swencten[17] the wrecce men of the land mid[18] castel-
weorces. Thá the castles waren maked, thá fylden hi mid
yvele men. Thá namen hí thá men the[19] hí wenden[20] thæt
aní god hefden,[21] bathe be nihte and be dæics. Me[22] henged
(they) up bi the fét, and smoked heom mid ful[23] smoke : me

nounced long. Attention to this fact will more easily enable
the student, in pronouncing old English, to arrive at the meaning of the words.

[1] baptism.　　　　　　[2] in.　　　　　　[3] third-wise.
[4] wo two (Saxon dual).　　　　[5] both.
[6] rule-book (Germ. regel).　　[7] follow (Germ. folgen).
[8] Canon's.　　[9] rank.　　[10] as.　　　[11] performed.
[12] wended (turned).　　[13] holy (Germ. heilig).
[14] Lord.　　[15] lent.　　[16] advantage.
[17] swinked (vexed).　　[18] with (Germ. mit).
[19] whom.　　[20] weened (thought).
[21] had.　　[22] men.　　[23] foul.

dide cnotted[1] strenges abútan[2] here hæved, and writhen[3] to thæt hit gæde[4] to the hærnes.[5]

* * * * * * *

On this yær wærd the King Stephen did, and bebyried there; his wif and his sune wæron bebyried æt Tauresfeld. That ministre[6] hí makiden.[7] Thá the king was ded, thá was the eorl beionde sæ, and ne[8] durste nan[9] man don other bute god for the micel eie[10] of him. Thá he to Engelande come, thá was he underfangen[11] mid micel wortscipe; and to king bletcæd[12] in Lundine, on the Sunnen dæi beforen mid-winter-dæi.

LORD'S PRAYER IN SAXON.

Fæder ure, ther the eart on heofenum, si thin nama gehalgod; to become thin rice;[13] geweordhe thin willa on eorthan swa swa on heofenum. Urne[14] ge[15] dæghwamlican hlaf[16] syle[17] us to-dæg, and forgyf us ure gyltas swa swa we forgifadh urum gyltendum, and ne gelæde thu us on costnunge,[18] ac alys[19] us of yfle.

FROM.'THA HALGAN GODSPEL.'

On fruman waes Word, and thaet Word waes mid Gode, and God waes thaet Word. Thaet waes on fruman mid Gode. Ealle thing waeron geworhte thurh hyne; and nan thing waes geworht butan him. Thaet waes líf the on him geworht waes, and thaet líf waes manna leoht. And thaet leoht lyht on thystrum; and thystro thaet ne genamon. Man waes fram Gode asend, thaes nama waes Johannes. Thes cóm to gewitnesse, thaet he gewitnesse cythde be tham Leohte, thaet ealle men thurh hyne gelyfdon. Naes he Leoht, ac thaet he gewitnesse forth-baere be tham

---

[1] knotted.   [2] about.   [3] writhed (twisted).
[4] goed (went).   [5] brain (Germ. gehirn).   [6] minster.
[7] made.   [8] not.   [9] no (double negative).
[10] awe.   [11] received (Germ. empfangen).
[12] blessed (consecrated).
[13] rice = Germ. reich; retained in our present word bishopric.
[14] our.   [15] also.   [16] loaf.   [17] give.
[18] temptation.   [19] deliver.

Leohte. Soth Leoht waes, thaet onlyht aelcne cumendne man on thysne middan-eard. He waes on middan-earde, und middan-eard waes geworht thurh hine, and middan-eard hine ne gecneow. To his agenum he cóm, and hig hyne ne underfengon. Sothliche swa hwylce swa hine underfengon, he sealde hym anweald thaet hig waeron Godes bearn, tham the gelyfath on his naman : tha ne synd acennede of blodum, ne of flaesces willan, ne of weres willan; ac hig synd of Gode acennede. And thaet word waes flaesc geworden, and eardode on us (and we gesawon hys wuldor, swylce án-cennedes wuldor of Faeder), thaet waes ful mid gyfe and sothfaestnysse.

ALFRED THE GREAT. A.D. 890.

(A translation from 'Boethius de Consolatione Philosophiæ,' a book Alfred is said to have always carried in his pocket.)

We sculon get, of ealdum[1] leasum[2] spellum,[3] the[4] sum bispell[5] reccan.[6] Hit gelamp[7] gió,[8] thaette án hearpere waes, on[9] thaere theode the Thracia hatte.[10] Thaes náma waes Orfeus. He haefde an switha[11] œnlic[12] wif. Sio waes haten Eurydice. Thá ongann monn secgan be[13] tham hearpere, thaet he mihte hearpian thaet se wudu[14] wagode[15] for tham swege,[16] and wilde deor[17] thaer wolden to-irnan[18] and standan swilce[19] hi tame waeron, swa stille, theáh he menn oththe hundes[20] with[21] eoden,[22] thaet hí hí[23] ná ne ouscunedon.[24]

Thá saedon hí thaet thaes hearperes wif sceolde acwelan,[25] and hire sawle mon sceolde laedan to helle.

[1] old.   [2] lying.   [3] tales (as Godspell).
[4] to thee.   [5] example.   [6] reckon (tell).
[7] happened.   [8] formerly.   [9] in.   [10] was called (hight).
[11] very.   [12] only.   [13] of.   [14] wood.
[15] wagged (moved).   [16] sound.
[17] deer, beasts (Germ. thier).   [18] run.   [19] so like (as if).
[20] hounds (dogs).   [21] against. [22] went.
[23] they, them.   [24] shunned. [25] be killed (die).